There was no doubt there would be a next strike

And perhaps another after that. Bolan had already considered trying to lure the enemy out into the open, away from the downtown hotels, but thus far he had no bargaining chips. That might change if he gained some new battlefield intelligence to help them make the next strike cleaner, more precise.

Bolan examined his companions, one face at a time. They were weary but willing, grim-faced and going for broke. He knew what his brother and Grimaldi were made of, and Bolan had seen enough of Keely Ross in action to figure that she wouldn't let him down. As for the aftermath—and anything that might go wrong with the hotel raid that night—they would simply have to live with it.

Bolan hoped he'd come out on the other side with everyone who'd joined him at the starting line. If not...

Well, there was always hell enough to go around.

MACK BOLAN ®
The Executioner

The Executioner®
Don Pendleton's

FLAMES OF FURY

The ORGCRIME Trilogy

BOOK II

A GOLD EAGLE BOOK FROM

WORLDWIDE®

TORONTO • NEW YORK • LONDON
AMSTERDAM • PARIS • SYDNEY • HAMBURG
STOCKHOLM • ATHENS • TOKYO • MILAN
MADRID • WARSAW • BUDAPEST • AUCKLAND

First edition August 2004
ISBN 0-373-64309-8

Special thanks and acknowledgment to
Mike Newton for his contribution to this work.

FLAMES OF FURY

Printed in U.S.A.

What we call real estate—the solid ground to build a house on—is the broad foundation on which nearly all the guilt of this world rests.

> —Nathaniel Hawthorne, 1804–1864
> *The House of the Seven Gables*

Property is theft.

> —Pierre-Joseph Proudhon, 1809–1865
> *What is Property?*

The enemy wants a piece of real estate to call his own. So be it. I have a special plot in mind. It's six feet long and six feet deep.

> —Mack Bolan

To America's fighting men and women in harm's way.
Stay strong. God keep.

Peninsula de Azuero, Panama

The rain forest was a second home to Mack Bolan. He had come of age in jungles, hunting men and being hunted in return. It was a life few men deliberately chose for themselves, but it suited him.

And it wasn't over yet.

Sometimes it felt like centuries since he had taken his first plunge into the primeval forest. That had been another war, another continent. Another life. He'd been as green as the luxuriant undergrowth in those days, but it hadn't taken long for Bolan to be bloodied and battle-hardened by experience.

He had been coming back to jungles ever since.

Some were like this one, replete with giant trees, stout vines and serpents dangling, the rank mulch of millennia beneath one's feet. Others were less verdant, cast from concrete, steel and glass, nary a blossom or blade of grass in sight, skies darkened by the noxious fumes of man. One jungle or the other, though, the predators were equally ruthless, deadly.

Given half a chance, they'd swallow the unwary traveler alive.

This day, however, Bolan and his two companions were the

predators. They'd traveled far in search of prey, using every means at their disposal to achieve the critical advantage of surprise. That didn't mean they would succeed, of course.

Pausing to check the compass and his watch, he thought, It won't be long.

Less than a mile, by Bolan's calculation, and the enemy would be within their grasp—or they would fall into his hands.

Bolan trusted his two companions with his life, which was the best that he could say for anyone. The trust came naturally where his brother—Johnny Gray to the world at large—was concerned. It was a bond of blood and loss that spanned most of their history together, which dated from before Johnny'd been old enough to shave. Bolan had done his best to keep Johnny out of his battles, but now reckoned there must be something in their genes.

Keely Ross was a whole different story. The brothers had encountered her by chance, learning she was working toward a common goal for the Department of Homeland Security. When Bolan and Johnny had arrived on the scene, she'd been slated for disposal by their common enemy. But Ross had pulled her own weight and then some in the death struggle that had followed and had been matching their pace ever since. This hike in the woods was no exception.

Bolan hoped they weren't about to get her killed.

It had been three hours since their insertion by a low-flying helicopter with Jack Grimaldi in the pilot's seat, and Bolan calculated that they should be almost close enough to smell the ether. He hadn't picked up a whiff yet. The drug refinery they intended to destroy was supposed to be up ahead. Three-quarters of a mile or less, north by northeast.

Their intel had been gleaned from CIA and DEA reports fleshed out through satellite surveillance photos and selected radio and cell phone intercepts compiled by the computer team at Stony Man Farm. But knowing where the coke was processed and preventing it were very different things. The fix was in with Panamanian officials where it mattered, and removing Manuel Noriega from the driver's seat had done little or nothing to staunch the flow of drugs through Panama to the United States and Canada.

Only the names and faces changed.

The game remained the same.

Ironically, most of the men who called the shots on drugs in Panama came from another continent entirely. Chinese influence permeated Panamanian society from top to bottom, fueled by powerhouse investments on both sides of the law. Diplomacy and normal commerce were a part of it, but the black market also thrived on the input of the sinister Triad societies—the Chinese Mafia.

That might have been enough to lure Bolan south, but there was more. The larger picture, which had been developing for months, had been pointed out to Bolan by the urgent summons from his brother. There was more at stake than Chinese mobsters shipping drugs into the States, but Bolan knew he didn't have the whole truth yet.

He meant to grab another piece of it soon.

Another twenty minutes passed and he could smell the cocaine plant. A blind man could have found it, but Bolan took his time, watching for traps and sentries in the bush.

No need to rush.

Their enemies weren't going anywhere—unless, perhaps, to Hell.

THEY HAD REHEARSED the plan a dozen times with maps and photographs, but Johnny didn't question why his brother took them through it one more time. Experience had taught him there was no such thing as too much preparation for a firefight, even when a soldier thought he knew it all.

They had it covered on the gear, at least. Their camouflage

fatigues were U.S. Army knockoffs with the tags removed for safety's sake. Each of them packed a Steyr AUG assault rifle, chosen for reliability and anonymity. Their sidearms were Beretta semiautomatics, found in military service from the United States to Israel, Italy and France—again, untraceable. Their frag grenades were Canadian C-13s, distinguished from the Swiss HG-85 only by an additional safety clip. The knives they carried could be found in any military surplus store on five continents.

"So, we're clear?" Bolan asked when he was finished.

"Crystal," Johnny answered.

"Got it," Keely Ross replied.

The plan was simple in conception. They would fan out to surround the cocaine plant as best they could with only three combatants. Johnny's target was the motor pool, a hundred yards to the northwest of where they stood. Bolan's target was the open-air lab itself, while Ross would hit the mess tent and raise Hell with the staff.

It wasn't foolproof, but from what he'd seen so far, Johnny thought they had a fair chance of pulling it off.

"Okay, let's move," Bolan said. They separated, moving toward their appointed targets. Johnny stayed alert for trip wires and lookouts, ready to rock with his AUG at the first sign of trouble. A mottled green viper slid across his path, but Johnny let it go. Snakes were the least of his troubles at this point.

The drug-processing plant's rolling stock consisted of two half-ton trucks, three open Jeeps, a beat-up Land Rover and two motorcycles rigged for off-road travel. The motor pool was unguarded as Johnny approached—or so it seemed—and the vehicle count gave no fix on the number of on-site personnel.

Most would be peasant grunt labor, he guessed, with a chemist or two and at least one supervisor always on the scene. Security would be twofold, to keep intruders out while at the same time to make sure no one in the plant sampled or ripped off the merchandise.

How many guns would be assigned to that detail?

He guessed that would depend on how secure the Triads felt here, in their home away from home. Pervasive corruption might encourage them to let down their guard, but much of Panama—and the Azuero district in particular—still had a frontier feel about it. There were rebels in the mountains, sometimes bandits on the highways, and a cagey smuggler would take pains to keep his product safe.

Enough guns, then, to make it touch-and-go.

There was nothing complicated about Johnny's assignment. He went down the line of vehicles with his blade, flattening tires, one after another. When he was finished, he worked his way back, dipping wicks into fuel tanks, leaving them ready for a spark to start the fireworks.

He was nearly finished, when a scuffling sound in the back of one covered truck startled him. Johnny recoiled as a denim-clad figure rose from the truck bed, stretching and yawning, then froze and blinked in surprise at the stranger in front of him. There was a pistol thrust in his belt, but sleep and shock slowed his response time.

Johnny reacted on instinct, reaching up to grab the sentry's shirt and haul him bodily across the tailgate, banging the man's knees in the process. Clubbing his adversary with an elbow, Johnny struck him a solid shot across the face and slammed him against the tailgate. Slumping, dazed, the young man still had strength enough to reach for his pistol and begin to draw it from his belt.

Johnny lashed out with his right foot against the other man's left knee, buckling the leg. Even so, the gun was in his adversary's hand as Johnny drew his fighting knife. He lunged, slapping at the sentry's gun arm with his own left. The knife blade found its mark, grating along a rib as it slid out of sight.

A keening sound escaped from his opponent's throat, but it was muffled by the gunshot as the lookout's trigger finger clenched reflexively. The bullet struck somewhere behind Johnny, as he withdrew the dripping blade then hacked across the dying shooter's wrist. It was too late to take the noise back, but the shooting was finished.

Johnny drew the knife across the sentry's windpipe, making sure the man couldn't cause any more trouble. He looked up from his work in time to see two men with automatic rifles run toward the motor pool. They hadn't seen him yet, but any second now—

He sheathed the knife and took a lighter from his pocket, bending to the nearest gasoline-soaked wick.

CHIANG KAI-SHIN HAD BEEN forewarned of trouble, but the gunshot still surprised him. After two days with no further news of conflict from the States—and none at all in Panama—he had begun to think that the warning was a false alarm, someone's overreaction to trouble between the Italians in Miami. Occasional bloodshed was the price of dealing in contraband. Indeed, it was one of the curses the joint enterprise might relieve, if all went well.

Another day or two without incident and Chiang would have relaxed his guard. He might even have dismissed his standby reinforcements.

But he hadn't done it yet.

When the first shot sounded, Chiang reached for his portable two-way radio. He didn't sound the alarm at once, because his guards were sometimes overanxious with their weapons. They shot snakes from time to time, on the perimeter, and human beings on the odd occasion when a wayward peasant strayed too close to his own good. Chiang did not chastise them on such occasions, since the snakes were often venomous and peasants had to learn their proper place. Still, he dispatched two members of his own elite contingent to discover what had happened.

Chiang watched from the shade of his command post. They had almost reached the motor pool when one of the trucks exploded with a sound that seemed to suck the air out of the forest, then expel it once again in rippling shock waves. Chiang was gaping at the fireball when the second truck went up, and then the Jeeps began to detonate like giant firecrackers in a display for Chinese New Year.

Chiang's hand trembled as he raised the radio and thumbed down the transmitter button, bellowing into the mouthpiece, "Raven flight! Move in! We're under fire!"

He gave the order twice, then let the button go and waited for his answer. Static whispered for a moment from the radio, before a tinny voice came back at him. "Message received. We're on the way."

Chiang felt like telling them to hurry but restrained himself. The reinforcements were professionals. They knew their job and wouldn't let him down.

Unless they came too late.

As if in answer to his thought, the sound of automatic weapons erupted behind him, from the compound's southernmost perimeter—and, seconds later, from the east. Because his guards were uniformly armed with Chinese Type 56 rifles—Beijing's carbon copy of the venerable AK-47—Chiang immediately knew the weapons must be wielded by outsiders, firing on the camp.

Again he felt the urge to chide his reinforcements, order them to hurry. But Chiang knew it would be useless. Helicopters needed a certain time to rise aloft, acquire their course, and race across the treetops. Nothing he could do or say would change the laws of physics.

Better, then, for Chiang Kai-shin to save himself.

He ducked back through the open doorway of his quarters,

reaching for the wall hook where a pistol belt hung waiting for him. Seconds later it was buckled into place around Chiang's narrow hips. He drew the pistol, a Type 59 copied in China from the Russian Makarov PM, and racked the slide to put a live round in the chamber. Thus prepared, he moved back to the door and risked a glance outside.

Chiang's men were firing now, no doubt about it, but the ones that he could see appeared to have no targets. They were shooting for the hell of it, spraying the trees as if the racket gave them courage—and perhaps it did. It could mean trouble, though, if they were still out of control when the elite team tried to land.

Cursing, Chiang moved into the open, grabbing first one man and then another, shaking them and shouting orders, cowing them by force of will. He forced them to remember who they were, and who was in command, but it took time.

And from the sounds of combat spreading all around him, Chiang Kai-shin thought time might be in short supply.

KEELY ROSS TRACKED a running target with her AUG, led him a yard or so, and knocked him sprawling with a 3-round burst of 5.56 mm bullets. She supposed it should've pained her conscience, shooting him that way without a warning to surrender, but she had no time for legal niceties. This wasn't the United States, her badge meant nothing here, and she was fighting for her life against the odds.

Ross found another mark, lined up her sights and took the shot. She didn't think about the shocked expression on her target's face, how young he looked, or anything at all that would distract her from her mission.

This was do or die, and the outcome hadn't been decided yet.

Her supervisor would've had a stroke if he'd known where she was, much less what she was doing. Avery Koontz had signed off on her action in the States, but Ross was fifteen hundred miles beyond her mandate now, and operating on the wrong side of the law. It didn't matter if the men she killed were narco-traffickers, because she had no legal duty or authority to deal with them in Panama.

But she'd made the choice to follow where her mission led her, and this jungle clearing was a part of it. If she survived the action, there'd be time to think about the consequences later.

If.

A bullet whispered past her face, reminding Ross that she had no time for soul-searching. Swiveling to face the threat, she caught a Chinese gunman lining up another shot and dropped him with a short burst to the chest.

She wasn't keeping score, but these men were her enemies. More to the point, her comrades—known to her as Johnny Gray and Matt Cooper—seemed to think the Triad angle might reveal the targets who had slipped away from them in Florida. Ross wasn't altogether sure she bought it, but right now this seemed to be the only game in town.

Ross paused. Behind the sounds of gunfire and the crackling of flames as they devoured the motor pool, a noise wormed its way into her consciousness, demanding her attention. Ross couldn't place it for a moment, then the choppy sound sparked mental images and she reached up to key her headset microphone.

"I hear a chopper," she warned her companions. "Could be more than one."

After a heartbeat's hesitation, Johnny's voice came back at her. "I hear them, too," he said. "Sounds like a couple, anyway."

Ross didn't bother spelling out the obvious—that any helicopters headed for the jungle factory could only be hostile. Instead she asked, "What do we do?"

Cooper answered through the small earpiece. "Fall back," he told her, "to Position D. We'll go from there."

"Roger that," Ross responded.

Position D was on the north rim of the compound, 150 yards distant as the parrot flew from Ross's vantage point. It was more than twice that distance if she worked her way around the camp perimeter under cover. Anything could happen to her if she took the long way. Cutting corners through the compound, though, she stood a greater chance of being shot—or leading hostiles to the rally point and her companions.

They had discussed the possibility of reinforcements, of a trap, but Ross hadn't considered it too seriously. Even now, she didn't know if that was what the choppers meant. It could be a coincidence—the compound's weekly food delivery, for instance, or a bunch of hookers flying down from Santiago to amuse the staff.

Uh-huh, she thought. And I'm Eva Peron.

The choppers meant trouble, no question about it. All that remained to be seen was what kind of bad news they were carrying, and how bad the trouble would be.

Ross got moving.

The others would be heading for Position D by now and she didn't intend to slow them down. It was the first promise she'd made when they were trying to decide if she should join them on the jaunt to Panama: no slacking and no special treatment.

It was time to hustle, and she saw only one way to make it in time. Right through the middle of the camp. It was a risk she'd have to take, and anyone who tried to block her path or follow her was marked for death.

Teeth clenched, her finger on the Steyr's trigger, Keely Ross burst out of cover, running for her life.

BOLAN REALIZED there were at least two helicopters, and they were too damned close for comfort. He barely registered the Triad gunman stepping out in front of him. A shadow rose from behind a tree on Bolan's left, before his AUG stuttered a 3-round burst and cut the stranger down.

Behind him, shouts and gunfire warned Bolan of hunters on his trail. He ducked behind another looming tree and palmed one of the C-13 frag grenades, hooking the safety pin loose with his thumb. He waited, counting off the seconds as the roar of the approaching choppers made tracking his enemies more difficult.

Go for it!

Bolan pitched the grenade with a looping side-arm toss around the tree trunk, estimating the distance, hoping that they wouldn't see the trap in time to save themselves. The blast was somewhat muffled by surrounding undergrowth, but not the screams or the sounds of shrapnel slapping into trees.

When Bolan stepped from cover, only one of his pursuers was still upright, standing with one arm braced against a nearby tree, the other hanging limp and bloody at his side. Another man was kneeling in the churned-up mulch of dirt and leaves; a third lay silent, stretched out on his back some distance from the other two. The standing figure was Chinese, the other two Hispanic, maybe Panamanian.

Two short bursts from the AUG resolved the issue of their nationality and their purpose at the compound, sending them in tandem to their last reward or punishment.

The choppers thundered past above his head and to his left, circling above the open ground around the drug plant. Bolan recognized the matched pair of Bell 412 choppers that had evolved from the UH-1 Hueys once so common in U.S. military service. The 412 was longer and slimmer than its predecessor, with a four-bladed rotor to improve handling and decrease fuselage vibration, but it still carried up to a dozen passengers beside the two-man crew. As the chopper banked away from him, a glimpse through one of the open cargo bays showed Bolan a line of stern faces and rifles.

Reinforcements.

Bolan didn't wait to watch the troops unload, nor did he try to bring the choppers down. They were within range of his rifle, and he might've raised hell with the passengers at least, but he was focused on his comrades and their chances of getting out alive to fight another day.

The jungle raid was starting to unravel; there'd been no chance to question anyone in charge and thereby make the effort worth their while.

Not quite.

Before he turned to leave, Bolan reached down and keyed the radio-remote detonator clipped to his web belt. A silent signal, undeterred by the chaos, beamed across the compound to find the C-4 charge he'd left beside the chemical storage hut. It detonated with a concussive force that sent a tongue of flame leaping to treetop height before it fell back to its source and started to devour the camp.

Bolan moved on, seeking his brother and the woman who had traveled with them to this little bit of Hell on Earth. He hoped that all of them could slip away unseen and find another way to track their quarry.

Of course, they'd have to be alive to do the job.

He reached Position D a moment later, finding Johnny there ahead of him. Their eyes locked and a silent question passed between them, but before they had a chance to speak, a thrashing in the undergrowth alerted them to company arriving on the scene. Both men, both weapons, swiveled toward the sound in unison.

"Don't shoot, okay?" said Keely Ross, emerging from the wall of greenery.

"You cut through camp?" asked Johnny.

"I was in a hurry," she replied. "Am I the only one who saw the whirlybirds?"

"I saw them," Bolan answered, "and the men they're carrying. We need to go before they get a fix on us."

"Seems like a shame," Ross said, "to come this far for nothing."

Bolan shrugged. "We rolled the dice. We only get another chance if we're alive."

Ross nodded briskly.

And so they ran. Their course had been determined in advance, confirmed now by the compass Bolan carried and his keen sense of direction. They had covered something like a hundred yards when Bolan heard the choppers lifting off again. He wasn't sure what to expect—a search pattern, perhaps—but it was no great shock when they drew closer, as if following his party from above.

"Dammit! How did they find our trail so fast?" called Johnny from behind him.

Bolan answered without breaking stride. "They haven't. I was followed halfway to the rendezvous and had to take some people out. Best guess, they found the bodies and extrapolated."

"Great!"

"It's done," the Executioner replied. "Pick up the pace before they overtake—"

The helicopters passed above them, whipping humid air—and held that course, moving away as if the pilots thought the raiders had been traveling by jet instead of slogging through the rain forest on foot.

"What the hell?" asked Keely Ross.

Small favors, Bolan thought, but he knew there had to be a stormy cloud behind the silver lining. He couldn't believe their enemies would be so foolish. It must be some kind of trap.

But what?

Safety lay beyond the point where the two helicopters had already passed out of sight and hearing, to the north. They had no choice but to continue on their way to see what waited for them up ahead.

CHIANG KAI-SHIN WAS snapping orders at the disheveled survivors of his command before the twin helicopters vanished from sight beyond the treetops. Some had already set off in pursuit of the enemy, traveling overland on foot, and there was no end of urgent work for those who remained. The compound was in disarray, some of its buildings flattened and incinerated, others badly damaged. It appeared that all their vehicles had been destroyed. Chiang didn't know how many of his men were dead or wounded yet—or of the latter, who would manage to survive.

Too many questions, with the raiders still at large.

But not for long, he thought, managing to produce a smile of sorts. The chase was on, and Chiang would have them yet. He only hoped that one or more was brought before him still alive, for questioning.

It would be helpful—and he would derive enjoyment from the music of their screams.

Unfortunately he could not delay his report of the attack to Sun Zu-Wang in Panama City.

Sun had warned Chiang of possible danger, based on recent events to the north, in Florida and elsewhere. He had placed extra troops and helicopters at Chiang's disposal, while explaining that they probably wouldn't be needed. It was a precaution, nothing more or less—but now it would pay dividends.

Chiang hoped so, anyway.

Would Sun be angry that he'd kept the reinforcements at a distance from the plant, instead of staking them out on the perimeter? They had agreed on Chiang's final strategy, of course, but that didn't mean he'd be absolved from guilt for its failure. *Someone* was responsible for every failure, every setback in life, and the guilty were frequently punished. In that respect, the Triads were often more efficient—and certainly more ruthless—than the society that hosted them.

Would Chiang be the scapegoat for today's disaster?

There was no time like the present to find out.

He finished assigning the burial details, then moved toward his quarters. The small building was mostly unscathed, though a few random bullets had peppered the walls and drilled one of the Plexiglas windows. Inside, Chiang found his personal gear undamaged, except where one slug had creased the sleeve of a jacket hanging from a wall hook.

Chiang's radio, a larger version of the two-way walkie-talkie he carried, sat waiting for him on stand beside his metal desk. A part of Chiang had hoped it might be shattered, thus forestalling the inevitable, but he saw there'd be no respite from the morning's litany of trouble.

Chiang sat in front of the radio and switched the power on, then checked the dials to confirm Sun's frequency. It was already set, because he rarely spoke to anyone else from the compound, but the stall bought him another fifteen seconds of peace before the storm.

Chiang raised the microphone and spoke Sun's call letters, using the code name they'd agreed upon months earlier. It was not Sun himself who answered on the third attempt, but rather one of his security officers. Chiang was tempted to leave a brief message and sign off the air, but he knew that would only make things worse for himself.

He must give Sun the news directly and then take his medicine, no matter how bitter it turned out to be.

Chiang told the security man it was urgent, then waited while someone went off to fetch Sun. It seemed to take forever, but the small clock built into the radio receiver told him less than a minute had passed before Sun's voice came on the air.

"What is it, Viper Two?" Sun asked without preamble.

"Sir," Chiang said, "the difficulty we discussed has sadly come to pass."

Bolan's team was a mile from their target and making fair time when it started to rain. Not the gentle sprinkling of an early summer shower in the drab New England town where he'd been raised, but the kind of steaming deluge that gave the rain forest its name. One moment they were running through sunshine and shade, the next they were staggered by gallons of water cascading from heaven as if a trapdoor had opened in the bottom of some vast celestial sea.

Bolan ran through the cascade and called to the others behind him, demanding that they keep pace through the downpour, regardless of earth turned to slippery mud underfoot. He ran because their lives depended on it and a rest stop anywhere along the way could end in sudden death.

He couldn't hear the helicopters in the hissing downpour, didn't know if they'd passed back along their route or were circling somewhere overhead, riding out the storm and waiting for another chance to find their prey.

One consolation was the fact that any foot pursuers would be slowed by the rain as much as Bolan and his two companions. Even a native of the forest couldn't do much better when the very earth was sluiced out from beneath his feet.

They slipped and fell while climbing even gentle slopes,

fell yet again and slid along the down-slopes on their backsides. Running on level ground was grunt work, squinting through the sheets of rain and praying that the rain wouldn't send an arboreal viper thrashing to earth—or down someone's collar.

They were soaked to the skin within seconds, chilled to the bone moments later despite the forest's mean temperature of seventy-five degrees Fahrenheit. The rain plastered hair to scalps and foreheads, drenched equipment and found its way inside boots. Mud sucked at those boots and the feet inside them, slowing progress to the crawl of a frustration dream.

The good news, Bolan thought, was that the hunters stalking them in this nightmare weren't supernatural. They were taking the very same beating, slogging through the same muck and mud, while the storm washed away any tracks left by Bolan's team. There was even a chance, however remote, that the trackers might get lost or turn back.

Bolan never doubted their existence, though. He knew the hunters were back there, somewhere. He hadn't killed enough of the enemy in camp to prevent them from giving chase. Which meant he'd have to kill more of them on the trail.

All he needed was some warning and a half decent shot. Of course, the forest and the elements might not provide those opportunities.

In which case, he would simply have to do the best he could with what he had.

Despite his best intentions, Bolan stopped a hundred yards into the storm. He pressed against one of the forest giants in the hope its boughs would shelter him, but the relief was minimal. Johnny and Keely Ross stood close by so they wouldn't have to shout.

"You think we'll lose them?" Johnny asked.

"Don't count on it."

Ross shook her head like a bedraggled, rain-soaked puppy.

"I'll be damned if I could see them twenty feet away," she groused.

"You'll hear them, if they find us," Bolan promised. "I have a hunch we're losing ground right now. We don't know where the choppers went, or if they dropped insertion teams somewhere ahead to cut us off."

"Dammit!" The slump of Ross's shoulders eloquently spoke of her despair.

"It's just a possibility," Bolan continued, "but they were ready with backup and may have a plan. We need to stay focused in all directions. If the air search missed us, fine. But we can't take a thing for granted while we're still being pursued."

"So what's the plan?" asked Johnny.

"Hold a steady double-time until we've covered two more miles, at least. If there's no one in front of us by then, we stop and lay a trap."

"Guess that would be a water trap," said Ross.

"I'll take whatever edge there is," Bolan responded. "For the moment, though, can everybody run?"

"Watch me," Ross answered grimly.

"Set the pace," said Johnny.

"Right. Let's do it, then."

He did as Johnny'd asked him, setting a pace that was steady and strong, without sprinting toward total collapse. They were covering ground, but not recklessly. With Bolan on point, there was still a decent chance of detecting an ambush before they fell into a trap.

Or so he hoped.

DAVID CHIN WAS GRATEFUL when the rain slacked off and the jungle began to steam once again in the afternoon heat. There'd been a moment, when the helicopters dropped his team off in a clearing four miles north of the plant, when he'd thought the combination of pouring water and thrashing rotor wash would leave him helpless, but the moment passed and he was in control once more.

His fifteen men, all camo-clad and armed with automatic weapons, looked to Chin for inspiration and commands. He'd briefed them on the plan while they were airborne: they were meant to head off the raiders, since Chiang Kai-shin hadn't been able to confine them in the compound. Bodies and other evidence showed that the enemy was fleeing northward, hence their leap to get ahead and set a trap across the trail. A smaller team would come along behind their quarry and cut off retreat.

Chin's first executive decision had been forced upon him when he discovered there *was* no trail, just trackless forest with torrential rain pouring from leaden skies and turning all below into a leafy porridge. Still, they had a solid fix on the direction of their enemy's retreat, and Chin proceeded with the drop on schedule.

Whatever happened after that, no one could say he'd failed for lack of courage or initiative.

Instead of staking out the nonexistent trail, he'd briefed his soldiers on the backup plan, making it up as he went along. They knew the enemy's starting point, had his route of march more or less plotted, and it should be possible to find the targets by fanning out, moving cautiously southward until contact had been achieved.

Unless the enemy changed course somewhere along the way, confounding all of them. It was a possibility that haunted Chin, because there weren't enough men in his team—in all of Panama, for that matter—to isolate the whole peninsula and sweep it yard by yard.

Besides, Chin had been entrusted with the task. It was his job and no one else's. He could not seek help, and if he failed, it would be his responsibility alone.

Chin knew there were two ways to blow a job like this. In one scenario the enemy slipped past him, unobserved, and he was forced to go back empty-handed. In the other, Chin met the enemy but failed to stop him, beaten in the field by strangers. Under the circumstances, Chin imagined either form of failure would mean death.

His men fanned out on Chin's command and started working southward, toward the plant. They kept a constant interval of thirty feet between them, thus maintaining visibility while covering a skirmish line nearly five hundred feet across. There were some problems, naturally: one soldier tangled with a ten-foot boa, while another stepped into a rushing stream and washed ashore a hundred yards downrange. Still, they were making progress and Chin thought they had a decent chance of intercepting their quarry.

Chin was a city boy at heart. Despite his training in guerrilla warfare with the People's Revolutionary Army, he had grown up in Guangzhou and made his way to Hong Kong a year after control reverted to mainland authorities. He had joined the Triad there, feeling that he had found real kinship for the first time in his life. There had been no regrets, whatever Chin was told to do, until he'd been transferred to Panama.

He'd recognized the golden opportunity and wouldn't have considered balking when the travel order came, but Chin couldn't help regretting that he had to leave Hong Kong, Macao, Kowloon—the world he'd come to claim as his—for *this*.

A rattle of gunfire to his left froze Chin in his tracks. He resisted the urge to shout questions and orders, waiting to learn if the shooting meant contact or signaled an outbreak of panic. His men should be tougher and wiser than that. If one of them was firing at shadows—

An explosion rocked the forest, shrapnel ripping leaves and fronds to tatters.

Chin broke the line and rushed toward the source of the blast, sidestepping roots and vines that could easily trip him, ducking under branches that were draped with moss and possibly with snakes. He didn't care about reptiles or insects now. Chin's targets were within his grasp.

And he would die before he let them slip away.

AT THE FIRST SOUND of firing, Keely Ross lunged for the cover of a giant tree that had fallen in some other rainstorm, its gnarled roots undermined and twisted free of the yielding earth. It was six or seven feet in diameter at the base, granting plenty of cover, but Ross couldn't see over the top as gunfire sputtered through the jungle, so she had to peer between the roots that sprawled like frozen tentacles.

She couldn't see Cooper, but she caught a glimpse of Johnny Gray crouched beside another tree and firing through a wall of gray-green ferns. The winks of muzzle flashes marked a few of their enemies, but from the sounds of battle all around her, Ross knew there were more than two or three guns in the ambush party.

Ross slipped out of cover, crawling on her belly through the muck, seeking a target. She found one seconds later, when two figures rose from hiding on her right front, scuttling through the gloom as they advanced. It seemed to Ross that they were bent on flanking Johnny, hoping they could take him from behind.

Ross unclipped one of the grenades from her combat webbing. It was covered with mud, but that didn't matter. She hooked the safety pin's ring to a straggling root, wrenched it loose, and putting everything she had behind the pitch, lobbed the grenade overhand toward the two adversaries.

It was a decent effort. Even falling slightly short, the lethal egg surprised the creeping gunmen, distracting them for the two or three seconds it took for the chemical fuse to burn down. The explosion seemed muffled, but still loud enough to shake new streams of water from rain-laden bushes and trees. A geyser of mud and shredded foliage shot up between

the shadow soldiers, taking both of them down as it fell back
to earth. Ross watched for a moment, ready for one of them
to rise, but both lay still and silent.

The firing built to a crescendo on all sides. Ross crept a little further out from cover, leading with her AUG, and in another moment saw the blinking muzzle flashes of her enemies.
She couldn't see their faces, but Ross knew they meant to kill
her and she didn't need instruction on the one and only viable response.

The Steyr used transparent plastic magazines, so there was
never any doubt about how many rounds remained at any
given time. Ross had replaced her AUG's half-empty mag
while on the run, before the downpour hit, and she was ready
to do battle now. Her weapon had a built-in flash suppressor,
doubling as a grenade launcher, but Ross had never tested either function and she wasn't certain how much cover it would
offer when she started pouring fire into her enemies' positions.

At the next muzzle flash she stroked a 4-round burst into
the undergrowth from twenty yards away. Ross saw a figure
lurch and swing around, the muzzle of a weapon wavering,
but she fired again and put the sniper down. Ross couldn't say
if he was dead or not, but he was definitely hit, and others now
demanded her attention.

She swung toward the next mark in line, half expecting the
gunner to take her out first, but her luck was holding. The rifleman was still focused on Johnny, who in turn had been
forced to change his position, ducking and retreating under
fire. Johnny hadn't been hit yet, from what Ross could tell,
but she guessed it was only a matter of time.

She peered through the AUG's optical sight, watching her
target loom into closer relief. It wouldn't do for long-range
sniper work, but at this range it gave Ross an edge she could
use. The shooter's face was cast in profile, smeared with war
paint that distorted lines and shadows.

The Steyr had no fire-selector switch. Single shots and automatic fire were controlled solely by pressure on the rifle trigger. Ross took it easy this time, lightly curling her finger, holding the weapon rock-steady with her elbows braced in the mud. The bullpup design absorbed most of the recoil, but the sight still jerked a fraction of an inch and blurred her vision as a bullet closed the gap between marksman and target.

The painted rifleman slumped backward, as if he'd decided it was too much work to hold his weapon level and he needed to relax a moment in the shade—but then he kept on going, toppling out of view, feet rising, kicking once at empty air before the legs in turn went slack and dropped from sight.

Two down.

How many left?

From the continued firing up and down a skirmish line she couldn't see, Ross knew they still had work to do. Whether she'd live to see the job completed was something she could only guess at, but she had to try.

And in the process, she supposed it wouldn't hurt to pray.

JOHNNY GRAY WASN'T SURE who'd taken down the snipers, but he reckoned thanks could wait. In front of him he saw half a dozen muzzle flashes winking from the forest shadows, ever shifting, none of his opponents trusting one location for security. They had Kalashnikovs, but the higher-pitched answer from 5.56 mm rifles on either flank told him that his brother and Ross were still in the fight.

They had a chance, but the odds were against them and any small error could tip them lethally in favor of the enemy.

Johnny checked his AUG's transparent magazine, found it still half full, and picked another target from the shifting line of muzzle flashes. They were firing on his old position at the moment, unaware that he had moved while one of his com-

rades had engaged the flanking snipers. With any luck, that
shift might be the slim advantage he required to save himself.

He marked a muzzle flash, then waited for the shooter to
relocate, darting through the murk from one tree to another.
Johnny caught him halfway there and stitched him with a rising burst that spun his target like a dancing dervish before he
collapsed.

Move now!

They had his fix again, but Johnny dodged the probing fire
and wriggled through the dripping ferns another ten or fifteen
feet before he paused to scan for targets. Every move released
another shower on his head, but he was used to it by now. His
enemies were in the same boat, squelching mud with every
step, soaked to the skin and fighting in misery.

The choppers must've dropped them, he decided, but did
that mean no pursuers were advancing from behind? He
couldn't make that leap of faith, but Johnny hoped the weather
had retarded any trackers moving overland, while the helicopters took the ambush party ahead. If they were trapped between two hostile forces at the moment, it might prove too
much even for Johnny's brother to finesse.

Forget about the "maybes," dammit. Fight!

He took his own advice and caught a couple of his adversaries on the move. One zigzagged from one tree to the next,
while the other bulled ahead and made a beeline for the point
he had in mind. Johnny couldn't resist the easy mark. A short
burst cut the legs from under the man, before a second kept
him down for good.

The other shooter saw his comrade fall and marked the
source of lethal fire. Retaliating with a spray of bullets from
the hip, he veered off course and rushed toward Johnny's hiding place behind a jagged stump. It wasn't smart, but anger
and conviction that he'd never reach another sanctuary drove
the gunman to a desperate attack.

He nearly made it work.

A spray of bullets peppered Johnny's cover, ripping slivers from the rotted wood and hurling them into his face. He bellied down, letting the storm pass overhead, and fired back at his charging adversary from a worm's-eye view. A rising burst of 5.56 mm tumblers raked the shooter from knees to sternum, picking him up in midstride and slamming him down on his back.

Johnny waited another moment, half expecting the soldier to spring erect and continue the fight, but the enemy's strength had run out through his wounds. A shudder racked the prostrate form, then he lay still.

But Johnny still had other armed opponents in the forest, looking for a chance to kill him. His brother and Keely Ross were fighting for their lives on either side of him, cut off from one another by the ebb and flow of battle. And if his suspicion about hunters from the south turned out to be correct...

There was no time to waste.

The Steyr's magazine was almost empty now. Johnny removed it, took a fresh one from his bandoleer and slipped it into place. A sudden lull in firing close at hand let him pick out the subtle noises of advancing enemies, creeping upon him through the undergrowth. It sounded like a pincer movement in the making, at least one on either side of him and closing in.

He couldn't fire in both directions simultaneously, but that didn't make him helpless to a rush by multiple attackers. Johnny eased a C-13 grenade from its position on his battle harness, pulled the pin and held the explosive ready in his left hand as he clutched the Steyr in his right.

"You want it," he whispered, "come and get it."

MICHAEL YOH HAD NOT complained when told to lead a party of pursuers from the drug plant, following the raiders overland. His force included seven of the Triad soldiers who had choppered in, and an equal number of defenders from the camp itself, hand-picked by Chiang Kai-shin. With numbers nearly equal to the ambush party that had flown ahead, Yoh thought they stood a decent chance of punishing the raiders without taking many casualties of their own.

But the rain had slowed them down, a monsoon that wiped out tracks in front of them and left the hunters bruised, dejected. Under different circumstances Yoh might have canceled the exercise, but he was worried by the thought of what would happen if they lost their human prey. Better to march straight on through Panama and try to lose himself in Costa Rica than to go back empty-handed and confront the wrath of Chiang and Sun Zu-Wang.

Yoh was not prepared to fail. The rain had stopped after a time, and they'd pressed on, holding a northern course despite the total lack of signs along the way. Yoh guessed their enemies would trust the storm to hide all traces of their passage, but he didn't think they would abandon their objective—whatever that was.

Escape, for the moment, he reckoned.

And beyond that?

Yoh didn't care what they were thinking, as long as he found them in time to prevent their escape. He'd been ordered to capture one of the raiders alive "if possible," but the drenching and aggravation he'd suffered predisposed him to slaughter. The runners were bound to resist, and when they did—

Gunfire ahead gave substance to his reverie. Yoh couldn't judge the distance well enough to guess how far they were from contact.

"Be ready!" he commanded of his troops. The men he knew stood easy, several of them smiling, while the others looked disgruntled. "Double-time!" Yoh snapped. "No stragglers!"

They set off ahead of him, the camp survivors eyeing Yoh

as if they feared some trick. He came along behind them, glowering each time one of them glanced across a shoulder to find out if Yoh was keeping pace. He didn't trust the strangers, had no faith in their ability or will to fight, and kept a finger ready on his weapon's trigger just in case they turned on him and tried to run away.

The battle sounds grew closer by the moment, as his troupe ran northward through the forest. Even with the tramping, grunts and muffled curses from his fighters, there was no mistaking automatic rifle fire or the occasional explosion of a hand grenade. Yoh knew it wouldn't be long now before—

Yoh knew they'd found the enemy when his point man started firing. As he closed the gap behind the last two men in line, a smoky thunderclap enveloped the front ranks of his detachment and his men began to scream.

"Find cover!" Yoh commanded, shoving at the riflemen when they faltered, plainly of a mind to turn and run. "Go on, you bastards!"

One of them swung toward him, leveling his weapon, but Yoh was faster. Lashing out, he slammed his rifle stock into the rebel's face, cracking his jaw. The man went down, whimpering, but Yoh took no chances. He shoved the muzzle deep into the weeper's ear and squeezed the trigger once.

"Who else?" he hissed at those who stood and gaped around him, staring at the corpse, its shattered skull and the blood and brains that stained Yoh's boots. "Who doesn't have the nerve to fight?"

They ran from him, but they were running toward the battlefront, as Yoh desired. If they were fearful, let it be of him and not the enemy. This way, he knew that they would fight to save themselves, if nothing else.

Yoh moved, past the twisted bodies of his point men, scorched and torn by shrapnel. Bullets whispered all around him, but he couldn't say which came from hostile guns and which were coming from the ambush party flown ahead to block the enemy's escape route. Either way, a hit could kill him, and he kept his head down, seeking cover as he went along.

This was Yoh's chance to prove himself, and he was not about to let it slip away.

Not when he had the enemy within his grasp.

THE REINFORCEMENTS TIPPED their hand by firing as they charged, before they had acquired a target in the murky forest. Bolan had responded with a frag grenade, thus giving them no muzzle flash to zero in on, and used his Steyr only after shrapnel and the shock wave took down the front ranks of his latest adversaries.

It could be worse, he thought. They could be pros who know their way around a jungle.

Even so, the new arrivals were not giving up without a fight. They laid down cover fire from automatic weapons— more Kalashnikovs, he noted—and those still on their feet fanned out in search of cover, wasting no time in the open. Bolan couldn't see enough of them to pick out faces, but he noted some of them were dressed like workers from the drug plant, while the rest wore camouflage fatigues.

And in a flash, he realized where the rest of the troops from the choppers had gone.

It wasn't a bad move, as strategy went, but the ground team had arrived too late to do their comrades much good. Bolan and his companions had already whittled the ambush party's strength by roughly two-thirds, and he heard Johnny taking more down as the new troupe advanced through the trees.

Bolan wasn't complacent—the enemy plan could still work, and he knew it—but the odds had tipped enough for him to catch his second wind.

He had two grenades left from the supply he'd carried into Panama that morning. They would have to be replaced if he survived, but there was no point keeping them for some future rainy day, when it was pouring lead around his ears right now.

Palming one of the two deadly orbs, Bolan primed it and pitched it downrange, toward the spot where several of his enemies had gone to ground behind a massive log. His aim was good. He saw the bomb bounce once, wobble along the broad beam of the log, then dip and disappear from sight.

One of the hidden riflemen sprang up and tried to run. Too late. The fiery blast enveloped him and launched him toward the treetops in an awkward tumbling posture, trailing smoke from tattered flesh and fabric. Bolan waited for the other men to surface, but all that issued from behind the log was a pathetic voice, keening in mortal pain.

Bolan scanned the field for other targets. Here and there, the undergrowth was moving as if with life of its own, marking the progress of gunners who feared to show themselves. They erred in thinking that a wall of ferns and weeds would shield them, though—a lesson Bolan swiftly taught them with short auto-bursts from his Steyr AUG. The bullets cut through leaves and stalks as if they had been fashioned out of tissue paper, finding flesh and bone beyond.

It wasn't Bolan's nature to keep score of the men he killed, but estimating losses on the battlefield was part of making war. The present situation was anomalous, because he hadn't known his adversaries' strength to start with, but he knew his team must be making headway with the number they'd already taken down.

And it was time to drop some more.

He checked the field behind him and saw his brother firing from behind a muddy ridge some distance to his left. Ross wasn't visible from Bolan's vantage point, but he could hear her weapon stuttering short bursts and knew she was still in the fight. Whatever happened in the next few moments, Johnny and the lady Fed had Bolan's back.

It helped him to decide that he should go on the offensive and attack.

Granted, it was a risky move, but any holding action came with built-in limitations that could get a soldier killed unless he was adaptable. The best defense was sometimes still a good offense, whether in football or a struggle to the death with no holds barred.

Bolan checked the Steyr's load and primed the last grenade. Drawing a long, deep breath, he surveyed the field around him, chose his course and the alternatives he could pursue if he came under deadly fire.

He fell upon his enemies without a word of warning, pitching the grenade ahead of him, already moving as it fell among them and exploded, rending flesh. The Steyr blazed a path in front of him, chopping soldiers down whether they rose to fight or tried to run away. Some never knew what hit them, while their comrades had a fleeting opportunity to cringe in fear before the warrior's wrath.

Somewhere between his first step and the last, the AUG ran out of ammunition and he drew the sleek Beretta from its holster, rapid-firing as he ran. Stray rounds plucked at his clothing, whispered in his ear, but panic spoiled the aim of those who tried to take him down.

He killed them all, and in the sudden ringing silence of the forest knew that Ross and Johnny had destroyed the ambush party at his back. Bolan was standing in a haze of battle smoke, reloading, when they found him in a glade surrounded by the dead.

"Looks like we're done," Johnny said.

"Done here," Bolan corrected him. "We've still got work to do."

"Let's do it, then," said Keely Ross. "And if I never see another forest, it'll be too soon."

3

Washington, D.C.

Hal Brognola lifted the telephone receiver midway through its second ring. It was his private line, no routing through his personal assistant in the outer office or the Justice Department switchboard downstairs. The black telephone had a built-in scrambler and an unlisted number known to fewer than two dozen people on the planet.

"Brognola," he announced into the mouthpiece. "It's your quarter."

"Make that balboa," his caller replied, naming the basic currency of Panama.

"You made it, then," Brognola said. The distant sound of Bolan's voice engendered a sense of relief.

"We're here."

He knew that much from Jack Grimaldi, who had flown them in. Brognola wanted more. "So, how's it going?"

"Not as smoothly as I hoped," the Executioner admitted. "We had unexpected company at our first stop and didn't really get a chance to demonstrate our products."

Even with the scrambler running, Bolan kept it cryptic.

Brognola appreciated the discretion, but he needed to know what had gone wrong.

"A reception committee?" he prodded.

"Two whirlybirds full," Bolan said. "They dropped in a few minutes after we did."

"You're thinking there's a leak?" The prospect made Brognola's blood run cold.

"More like forewarning," Bolan answered, relieving some of Brognola's tension. "We missed connections with a couple of the players in Miami, and they could have gone south. If they did, you can bet they've been talking to friends."

The players in question were Maxwell Reed, self-declared president-in-exile of a tiny Caribbean nation called Isla de Victoria, and a mercenary contractor named Garrett Tripp.

Aside from his role as statesman-at-large, Reed was also actively engaged in trying to recapture power on his island homeland. The vehicle for that return to glory was a private army called the Victorian Liberation Movement, trained and commanded in the field by Tripp and a team of mercenary officers. Such machinations were routine in Latin America, but this effort had raised some official eyebrows when Reed's financial links to the U.S. Mafia were discovered by chance.

Bolan had recently severed that connection, striking in Louisiana and Florida at the Cosa Nostra families involved, taking out some of Reed's mercs and rebels in the process. But Reed and Tripp had wriggled through the net. Stony Man's best efforts had failed to locate them, so far, but Panama was definitely on the shortlist of potential destinations.

And that meant—

"So it's not just a Sicilian thing?" Brognola asked, wary.

"Not if the Golden Triangle's involved."

Brognola caught the reference to the Triads and the Asian district that was at the heart of global opium-heroin traffic. Trends varied in narcotics trading, as in any other industry.

One year the bulk of heroin sold in the U.S. might come from Afghanistan, then Turkey or Mexico, but grade-A "China white" was the recognized standard for quality.

At least where soul-killing poison was concerned.

"I take it East met West today," Brognola said.

"They aren't sure who they met," Bolan replied, "but that's affirmative. Beijing is definitely on the scene."

Of course, Brognola thought. Chinese investments and advisers had been moving into Panama ever since the U.S. relinquished its hold on the famous trans-isthmus canal. Panama was a convenient source of raw materials and cheap labor for Chinese industrialists, as well as an established stop for drugs cycling through the western hemisphere.

"What's next?" Brognola asked.

He could almost *hear* Bolan shrug at the other end of the long-distance line. "We still have the same objectives," his old friend replied. "We just need another angle of attack. I'm working on it."

"You'll watch your back, I hope."

"Count on it. When we have something, I'll be in touch."

"Can't wait," Brognola said before the link was severed and the line went dead.

In Bolan's case, he knew that *angle of attack* was no simple figure of speech. The action had barely started in Panama.

And before it was finished, there'd be Hell to pay.

Panama City

THE HOTEL WAS A COMPROMISE. Bolan and his companions had agreed that four gringos renting a Panama City apartment on the eve of an all-out shooting war might provoke enough gossip to help their enemies track them down. So the team—including flyboy Jack Grimaldi, on standby to help as needed—had agreed to rent three rooms in a midpriced tourist hotel and hope for the best. It was Keely Ross's idea to bunk with Johnny, "throwing off the profile" as it were, and no one questioned the decision after Johnny had agreed.

Romance or its hasty equivalent was the last thing on Bolan's mind as he joined the group that evening; he trusted Johnny to think with the right head where matters of survival and their mission were concerned. Beyond that, it was none of his business and he didn't give the sleeping arrangements a second thought.

Assuming any of them got to sleep.

The other three were waiting in Grimaldi's third-floor room when Bolan returned from placing his call to Brognola from a pay phone. He knew public telephones were less likely to be tapped, though nothing was certain in Panama, where drugs or "national security" were concerned.

Grimaldi answered Bolan's knock and locked the door behind him. Nodding toward a double-duty portable radio that sat atop a nearby dresser, the pilot said, "I swept the place first thing. No bugs."

"Make that no microphones," Ross interjected. "I found a roach in the bathroom the size of Godzilla's kid brother."

"Welcome to the tropics," Johnny said, smiling.

"I've seen the tropics," Ross reminded him. "The sign out front called this place a hotel."

"What's new from Wonderland?" Grimaldi asked.

"Nothing, so far," Bolan replied. "There's still no word on Reed or Tripp. They're working on it, but I think we have a better chance of getting something off the street than they do from the airwaves."

"So, I guess it's razzle-dazzle time," Grimaldi quipped.

"Looks like."

"Somebody want to clue me in on that?" asked Ross.

"We need to rattle cages," Johnny told her. "Shake some people up. Maybe throw out some questions in a way they can't ignore."

"Like back on the peninsula?" This time her question had a doubtful tone.

"It doesn't always work the way we plan it," Bolan acknowledged. "If you've got a better plan—"

"Not me." She raised her hands in mock surrender. "I'm just saying, we're cut off from anything resembling help down here."

"Which means we'll have to help ourselves," Grimaldi said.

"Hardware?" asked Johnny.

"Hardware," Bolan said. "High-ticket items first."

"That's me," Grimaldi noted. "We've got wings and wheels. The cars are nothing fancy, but they're functional and won't attract undue attention on the street. Sky-wise, we've got the chopper standing by at the local airport under corporate cover. Give me a few hours' notice and I can pop next door for a Learjet 24-D. It's waiting at Puerto Limón."

"Next door" was Costa Rica. Bolan hoped they wouldn't have to send Grimaldi border-hopping, but he couldn't rule it out this early in the game. "Sounds good," he said after the pilot finished. "Copies of the car keys all around?"

"It's done."

"Okay. That brings us to the *other* hardware," Bolan said. "Is everybody happy with the AUGs and sidearms?"

Nods around the circle told him they were satisfied, but Bolan wasn't finished with his shopping list just yet.

"We'll need more ammo," he went on, "and more grenades. I've got a local small-arms source on tap that should be able to supply them. While we're at it, I've been thinking we could use a sniper piece, maybe a couple of the smaller SMGs for some variety."

"Rifle grenades?" asked Johnny. "I mean, since the Steyrs have the built-in launchers."

"Couldn't hurt to ask," Bolan agreed. "DeMitri's paying for it, anyway."

Joey DeMitri, until very recently, had been the syndicate's top dog in southern Florida. Bolan had smoked him in the blitz that should've led to Maxwell Reed but which had come up short. Before they left Miami, Bolan had doubled back to tap one of DeMitri's numbers banks to fund the next leg of their journey. He'd already spent the better part of sixty thousand dollars, but they had another two hundred large in the war chest before they needed to find another donor.

"You want some company for the shopping?" Johnny asked him.

"Got it covered," Bolan said as Grimaldi stood and drifted toward the door. "You two stick close and stay frosty. If anything goes wrong, we'll try to get a message back."

"Just watch it, eh?" Ross urged.

"No sweat," said Bolan as they filed out of Grimaldi's room. "Watching is what I do."

At least, until it's time to strike.

Washington, D.C.

Avery Koontz lit his fifth cigarette of the day, inhaled deeply, and blew a plume of smoke toward the humming fluorescent light fixtures overhead. He had been nagging maintenance about the hum since he'd moved in six months ago, but nothing had been done so far. Apparently his posting to the Department of Homeland Security was designed to relieve someone else's headaches, not his own.

But if they didn't fix the damned lights soon—

The trilling telephone interrupted Koontz's revenge fantasy. He put the images on hold and lifted the receiver, taking time enough with the move to allow himself another drag on the cigarette.

"Koontz, DHS," he said by way of greeting.

"Do you recognize my voice?" asked Keely Ross.

"Barely," he said, frowning. "You sound like somebody who used to work here."

"Someone who was placed on leave, if you recall."

"And how's that working out for you?" he asked.

"The way we left it," Ross replied, "I wasn't clear on whether updates were desired."

"I'm always in the market for some useful information," Koontz allowed, "but comebacks are a bitch."

"Tell me about it."

Hesitant to broach the subject, still he took a shot. "So, I assume this is long distance?"

"Getting longer all the time."

"I really shouldn't ask," he said.

"Try Panama."

Koontz frowned. "This line isn't the most secure, if you—"

"I'll hit the highlights," Ross said, interrupting him. "What you decide to do with it is your business."

"Okay." Koontz leaned across his desk and pressed a button on the base of his telephone to start taping the call. "Fire away."

"We got the tip on Panama before we left Miami," Ross informed him. "There was no time to connect with you before flight time, and we'd already had our little talk."

Dammit! Koontz thought. He'd have to edit the tape now, if he ever planned to use it against Ross. "I'm listening," he said.

"It wasn't much of a pointer," she told him. "But we figured, how hard can it be?"

"That's the question."

"Anyway, it turns out the Stateside mob isn't Reed's only source of dirty cash."

Double damn! Another name. Koontz killed the tape and keyed it to erase, knowing that any use he tried to make of it would be more trouble than it was worth.

"Who else?" he asked.

"So far, Chinese," Ross said.

"Triads?" Koontz drew on his cigarette again but didn't taste the smoke this time.

"Looks like it. And the way things are down here, with the black market traffic, who knows what else we'll turn up."

"I guess you know this goes so far beyond our brief, I can't begin to calculate the violations."

There was momentary silence on the other end before Ross said, "I've taken that into account. The job needs doing, and I'd never feel right if I walked away from it, you know?"

"Regardless of the cost?"

"Regardless, right."

Now *that* he could've used on tape, but it was too damned late. Koontz lunged across the desk and punched the button again in time to catch his own response.

"Well, Agent Ross," he said—and winced at the formality—"I hope you understand that no one from this office has been authorized to operate…where was it? Panama, I think you said?"

A moment later, when she answered, Ross's voice was rigid, almost brittle. "Yes, sir. I realize deniability takes precedence over achievement in most situations, but thanks for reminding me."

"You know I didn't mean—"

"Here's what I mean," she cut him off. "We have a chance to do some good here, maybe stop a war that's brewing on our doorstep or prevent some kind of drug cartel from overthrowing the elected government of Isla de Victoria. I'm going for it while the opportunity exists. Since you can't help, I'll spare you any further aggravation on the subject. How'd that be?"

"My point—"

"I got your point," Ross said. "Consider this my formal resignation, paperwork to follow when I have the time."

"Now, please—"

But he was talking to dead air. The link was severed, only

silence on the line but for the faint—imaginary?—hissing of the tape.

Son of a bitch!

He killed the recorder, cradled the receiver, and stubbed out his cigarette. Koontz had another lit within five seconds, craving nicotine to calm his jangling nerves.

The words *rogue agent* echoed in his mind. He imagined them appearing in a memo, then in headlines, finally on network television news. Koontz could've smoked a carton and it wouldn't have forestalled the headache he felt coming on.

Ross had been right about the benefits of plausible deniability, but that had value only in a case where operations had been unofficially condoned. She'd left him with a very different problem now, and Koontz knew that it could blow up in his face before long.

Rogue agent on the loose in Panama, he thought, *and doing God knows what with who knows who.*

That kind of difficulty had been known to end careers. He could've stopped her in the early days, all right, but now it was too late.

"Damn you!" he cursed the empty office.

Then he settled back and started thinking of a way to save his job in case the whole thing went to Hell.

Panama City

"SO, HAVE YOU USED this guy before?" Grimaldi asked when they were on the road.

"Friend of a friend," Bolan replied. "You know how it goes."

Grimaldi nodded, checking out the street scenes as he drove. It meant the dealer might've done contract work for the CIA, the DEA, or some other entity in the alphabet soup of U.S. intelligence agencies at one time or another, but that didn't put his mind at ease. Black market weapons vendors usually stayed in business by collaborating with authorities *and* simultaneously dealing with the other side—be it leftist guerrillas, rightwing death squads or run-of-the-mill *narcotraficantes*.

In short, when it came to buying and selling illicit hardware, there were no clean dealers and no safe deals.

"You're thinking it could be a trap," Bolan remarked.

"I hate it when you read my mind."

"It's just a chance we take," said Bolan, trying to console him. "If it starts to fall apart, we make a run for it. Every man for himself."

That wasn't true, of course. Bolan had never left a comrade hanging in his life, and never would. Grimaldi felt the same. They'd faced too many risks and enemies together in the past for either one of them to run out on the other now.

"Okay," Grimaldi said, pretending he believed the lie. "Just so I know what's what."

"Left here, I think," Bolan directed him.

Grimaldi waited for the traffic light to change, then made the turn. He kept an eye out for police and tails they might've picked up after leaving the hotel. They didn't seem to have a shadow yet, and he had swept the cars for bugs before he'd taken delivery.

So far, so good.

A tail would be irrelevant, however, if the dealer they were on their way to meet had been staked out—or if he was cooperating with their enemies. They wouldn't know for sure until they had stepped into the trap—by which time it would be too late.

Grimaldi shrugged off the worry and went back to scanning the sidewalks. He'd walked and flown into traps with Bolan before, and he'd done it with eyes wide open, knowing that one slip could cost him his life. Hell, in some of the capers they'd pulled off together, it wouldn't have taken a slip-up. A shift in the breeze or their luck could've done it, and neither would've been rolling through Panama City this evening, on their way to buy a carload of weapons, explosives and ammo.

"Something wrong?" Bolan asked him.

"Not yet. How much farther?"

"It should be a couple of blocks. Right turn here."

Grimaldi didn't ask how Bolan knew where they were going. One look at a map and he could name the streets from memory, reciting which ones ran north-south or east-west and which were one-way. Grimaldi hadn't caught him in a flub, through all the years of their acquaintance, and he doubted that he ever would.

"That's it," said Bolan, pointing to a jeweler's shop on his side of the street. The sign out front identified it as Gallardo's.

"Not a lot of parking on the street," Grimaldi noted. There were no spaces, in fact. He drove past, checking on the right for stakeout teams while Bolan watched the left. He spotted nothing obvious—no unmarked vans with tinted windows and too many radio antennas; no hard-eyed gorillas sitting in their cars at curbside—but that didn't mean the place was clean, by any means. There could be shooters waiting in the shop itself, or studying the street from any one of several hundred windows up and down the block.

Grimaldi circled in a holding pattern, waiting for a space to open at the curb, then finally gave up at Bolan's urging and pulled into a high-rise parking garage, two blocks north of Gallardo's. They wound up on the fifty level, one below the open roof, nosed in between a minivan and a Mercedes-Benz.

"That makes a long walk back," Grimaldi warned his friend.

"No sweat. If we get lucky, I can make the payoff while you come back for the car."

"Uh-huh."

"Relax," said Bolan as they stood together in the cavernous garage. "We're just two gringo tourists helping out with the economy."

"Sure thing." Grimaldi took his only consolation from the weight of the Beretta autoloader tucked into his belt. "Let's go do it, then," he said, "before I get so damned relaxed I fall asleep."

IT WAS A LONG WALK from the garage, but Bolan kept it casual. The pedestrians who passed them on the sidewalk didn't spare a second glance for Bolan or for Grimaldi; if they were under scrutiny from watchers anywhere along the street, he couldn't pick them out.

Gallardo's was a relatively modest shop with nothing but watches in the window facing the street. Bolan supposed that high-priced items might've tempted thieves to try a smash-and-grab attack, but he was not concerned with gems. The pieces he required were strictly functional, and they would not be on display for normal customers.

An electronic chime went off as they entered the shop, Bolan leading, while Grimaldi hung back and made a final check of the street for anyone with a sudden interest in their destination. At a headshake from the pilot, Bolan turned his full attention to the store and its proprietor.

"Luis Gallardo at your service, gentlemen!" The man approaching them with manicured hand outstretched was jovial, dressed for success in an expensive charcoal-colored suit that made his mane of snow-white hair seem even brighter by contrast. His smile had a glint on one side that might have been white gold or platinum.

"New customers," he said while grasping Bolan's hand and then Grimaldi's. "Tell me, please, how I may serve your every need."

"My uncle recommended you," Bolan replied.

A flicker of uneasiness passed fleetingly in the jeweler's eyes. "A referral? Excellent! Perhaps if I may know your uncle's name?"

"It's Samuel. I call him Sam."

"Of course." The smile remained in place, but it had lost its gleam. "A special friend and client, always. You require the *other* merchandise, I take it?"

"That's correct."

"Ah, well. It's nearly time for the siesta, as you see. It shouldn't hurt to close the shop a bit early, for privacy's sake." Suiting words to action, Gallardo stepped past Bolan to reverse a sign hanging on the shop's glass door. He turned three different locks, securing the door, then turned again to face Bolan and Grimaldi. "If you'll follow me, please?"

They trailed him past display cases, past the cash register, into a storeroom of sorts at the back. There, Gallardo opened what appeared to be a closet door and flicked a light switch, revealing steep wooden stairs. He led the way down to a basement that was air-conditioned from the shop above and cleaned frequently to keep its stock of special merchandise dust- and rust-free.

Assault rifles lined one wall of the cinder-block chamber, standing upright in racks with their muzzles aimed at the ceiling. Another wall had hooks for smaller weapons, submachine guns and pistols displayed like tools in a hardware store. Ammo cabinets lined a third wall, while two long tables occupied much of the floor, their surface and the floor beneath them heaped with various pieces of hardware including rocket launchers, grenades, an M-60 machine gun and more ammunition.

"So, gentlemen," Gallardo said, "what do you need?"

Bolan ran through their shopping list, collecting extra 5.56 mm ammo for the Steyr AUGs, 9 mm for their pistols, and more grenades—Austrian HG-86 minis, this time. For concealment, he picked out a matched pair of Spectre SMGs, the Italian wonder gun that measured less than fourteen inches with its stock folded, feeding 9 mm cartridges from a unique 50-round box magazine at a cyclic rate of 850 rpm. For the potential distance work, Bolan chose a Heckler & Koch PSG-1 sniper rifle chambered for 7.62 mm NATO ammo, with three extra 20-round mags.

"A princely arsenal," Gallardo said when Bolan finished collecting his wants. "Perhaps you'd also like to take an RPG, or some *plastique?*"

"Just what we've got," Bolan replied. "And we'll need duffel bags, of course."

"Of course—and, how you say it? On the house!"

The hardware wasn't a bargain, but Bolan saw no point in haggling over prices. Gallardo was less likely to betray them if they left him satisfied, with the potential for some future dealings, and the money was a giveaway in any case. When they had wrapped and bagged their purchases, Grimaldi went to fetch the car while Bolan and Gallardo lugged the guns upstairs. Based on his heavy breathing, Bolan guessed the jeweler wasn't used to lifting anything much heavier than bracelets and tiaras.

While they waited, Gallardo made small talk. "Will you be staying long in Panama?" he asked.

"It's hard to say," Bolan replied. "We have a job to do, but things come up. You know that story."

"Yes, indeed. If I can be of any further help to you, in any way at all."

"I don't see how. Unless…"

"Please, do not hesitate, *señor!*"

It was a gamble. Bolan frowned, then tossed the dice.

"I'm looking for a man named Maxwell Reed," he said. "Caribbean, a politician. You may be familiar with him from the news."

Gallardo blinked, too rapidly and too often for innocence, before he said, "I'm sorry, no. The name means nothing, I'm afraid."

"No sweat," Bolan replied, smiling. "It was a long shot, anyway."

A car pulled up outside, Grimaldi at the wheel. Gallardo held the door for Bolan as he exited the shop, relieved to see him go.

When they had stowed their purchases and merged with traffic once again, Grimaldi read the look on Bolan's face and asked, "What's up?"

"I left a message with our friend, for Reed," the Executioner explained. "No way of telling if he'll get it, though."

"What are we doing in the meantime, then?"

"You called it, Jack. It's razzle-dazzle time."

"THE TWO OF YOU ARE pretty close, I take it," Keely Ross remarked.

Johnny took another sip of local beer, one bottle each was the limit while they waited for his brother and Grimaldi to return. He hadn't seen the question coming in their conversation, and he wasn't sure exactly what to do with it.

"The two of who?" he asked, immediately feeling foolish.

"You and Matt," she answered, smiling patiently.

"I've known him quite a while," Johnny allowed.

"There's something," she continued. "Not quite a resemblance…"

It was Johnny's turn to smile. "I don't think we look anything alike." Not after all the plastic surgery Mack's had.

"It's something in the eyes," Ross said.

He waited for her to go on, thinking, My eyes are brown and his are blue. Where's this going?

She got there. "Maybe I'm imagining it, but it's like you've seen so much together—so much suffering, I guess—that now you share a common attitude."

"What attitude is that?"

"Not fatalistic," she decided, after some consideration. "Determined. Like you've drawn a line where bullshit stops and trouble starts."

"I don't start trouble," Johnny said.

"But you don't run from it. Most people run, in case you hadn't noticed."

"When did you stop running, Keely?"

Blushing, she replied, "Fairly recently, really. Once upon a time, I ran away from everything."

"I don't believe that for a minute," Johnny answered.

"Well, you should."

"No one discovers courage overnight. It may need cultivation, but you either have it or you don't. A coward doesn't change."

"You give me too much credit, Johnny."

"Maybe you don't give yourself enough."

"The brass at DHS has cut me loose, you know. I'm off the radar screen. That leaves it all to you and yours, whoever they are."

He ignored the implied question, reaching out to place a hand on Ross's shoulder. "Forget about it. You've already proved yourself. You made the team."

"So, why am I afraid right now?"

"Best guess? Because you're not an idiot."

"Don't tell me you and Matt get scared."

"I can only speak for myself," he replied, "I'm frightened every time the shooting starts."

"I don't believe it!"

"Well, you should. Fear isn't something you get rid of. You can work around it, though—like you've been doing."

"But—"

"No buts," he said, and leaned in close. Ross didn't pull away. Their lips met softly, melding, sparking passion deep inside—and pulled apart at the sound of a knock on the door.

Johnny moved to the peephole. His brother and Grimaldi stood outside. He nodded to Ross, then opened the door.

"You made good time," he said.

Grimaldi flashed a grin. "We're barely getting started, kid."

4

Sun Zu-Wang watched Maxwell Reed pacing in his study, pausing at the window on each pass and peering nervously outside. Reed had been in constant motion through the ninety minutes since his arrival, and it was starting to wear on Sun's nerves.

"Mr. President, please." Sun spoke softly, striving hard for reassurance. "I have guaranteed your safety unconditionally. No one can find you here."

"That's what they told me in Miami," Reed replied.

"*I* told you no such thing, before today."

Reed caught the change in tone and turned to face Sun from his place beside the window. When he spoke, the normal note of arrogant entitlement was missing from his voice. "I meant no disrespect to you, of course."

"I understand. Attempted murder can be so…unnerving."

Reed blinked at the choice of words. "Do you think these people followed me from the United States?"

"It's possible, of course," Sun said. "You must think so, yourself, or you would not be so uneasy."

Grim-faced, nodding, Reed admitted, "I cannot believe it is coincidence. And yet…"

"And yet," Sun finished for him, "why would they attack my men and not your own?"

"Exactly. If Halsey's people wanted me dead, they wouldn't waste time on Chinese. No offense, Mr. Sun."

"None taken," Sun assured him with a placid smile.

Grover Halsey, the current president of Isla de Victoria, was Reed's nemesis and the target of hostile machinations for the better part of two long years. He had good reason to retaliate and might consider it, if he could pin his target down. But Sun did not believe he was responsible for the attack that morning. From what Sun had seen of Caribbean warriors so far, the morning raid had been far too efficient, too professional, to pass for their handiwork.

Sun's momentary silence irritated Reed. He crossed the room, demanding, "What is it? What's wrong?"

"Simply a thought, Mr. President." It was difficult for Sun to use Reed's title without a note of mockery. "It occurs to me that the usurper Halsey may not be responsible for the recent unpleasantness."

"Not responsible?" Reed physically recoiled from the suggestion, snapping back to ask Sun, "Then who is?"

"Professionals of some sort, obviously. I'm concerned that ruling out U.S. involvement may have been a premature conclusion on the part of my esteemed colleagues in Florida."

"If so, it cost them their lives," Reed said.

"And while that may be punishment enough for negligence," Sun answered, "I'm afraid it doesn't help us at the moment."

"What do you suggest?" asked Reed.

"First, to maintain composure. Panic is the enemy within. It can defeat us even in the absence of an outside threat. Second, to learn as much as possible about our adversaries, so that when we meet again nothing is left to chance."

"And where shall we obtain this vital information?" Reed inquired.

"I'm not sure yet," Sun told his nervous guest. "No man in civilized society exists without some record filed away. The trick is knowing *who* and *what* to ask. When we discover that—"

"But what if there's no time?" Reed interrupted. He'd gone back to pacing, hands thrust in his pockets to conceal their trembling.

"Everything is still on schedule," Sun reminded him. "The soldiers who were lost can be replaced. The plan is still intact."

"But if it fails—"

"You will be taken care of as agreed," Sun promised.

That was true, at least—although Reed didn't know of the agreement reached between Sun and his comrades of convenience. If the mission failed for any reason, Maxell Reed would be eradicated as if he had never lived. No trace would linger to incriminate his backers, linking them to anything that had been done to liberate Reed's nation from its current government.

Reed didn't need to know about those plans. Not yet. There would be time enough to clue him in if anything went wrong before their day of victory.

And that might happen soon, unless Sun managed to identify and kill their stubbornly persistent enemies. If they continued on their present course—

"Not Halsey," Reed repeated, drifting off to stand beside the window, muttering. "Then who?"

"There is a possibility," Sun said, "that our opponents represent some agency of government."

"But when I asked DeMitri and Ruggero that—"

"They disagreed. I understand." Vincent Ruggero, until recently, had been the boss of the New Orleans Mafia. He had been killed along with Joe DeMitri, while protecting Reed in the United States. "We may assume their understanding of the situation was imperfect," Sun replied.

Reed was already shifting gears. "When you say government—"

"I mean some agency with the authority to carry out unpleasant tasks without involving heads of state. Most nations have at least one unit capable of such activities. Some, like the Russians and Americans, have several."

Reed stared at him, wide-eyed. "Russians? Americans? Why would they interfere? We *deal* with Russians. I was *living* in America, for God's sake."

"In the world of covert operations," Sun informed him, "different groups are frequently at odds. The FBI and CIA are classic examples, working at cross-purposes for decades, to the detriment of their nation. As for who may be responsible for these attacks and why, I must repeat that we can only wait and see."

"About security—"

"Fear not," Sun said. "You have my guarantee of safety for the moment, and full inquiry is in progress on the latest failure."

"But if Tripp cannot protect me—"

"Then he'll be removed," Sun promised, "and we'll find someone who can."

"I TELL YOU," Maxwell Reed declared, "that I do not feel safe with these Chinese."

His chief of staff, Merrill Harris, nodded earnestly and asked, "But, sir, what can we do?"

"Nothing, it seems—for now. But we must get word to the troops, explain the danger."

"But if Tripp cannot be trusted, sir—"

"Not Tripp," Reed spat, his mind churning with thoughts. "I mean our troops. The freedom fighters of Isla de Victoria!"

"Ah, yes. Of course, sir."

"They must persevere and know that loyalty will be honored in the end. Their sacrifices have not been in vain. They shall receive their just rewards as soon as we have seized control and thrown the traitors out."

"Yes, sir."

"The others, these vultures, believe they control me. Because they have the money and weapons I need to fulfill my destiny, they think I am their creature, a pawn to be moved as they will." Reed saw the frown on his companion's face, as if Harris harbored similar notions. "Well, let them believe it! They'll learn in the end how mistaken they were."

"As you say, sir."

"You doubt me, Merrill?"

"No, sir! Never!" Harris cringed, as if expecting to be struck. When Reed did not assault him, he relaxed a bit and said, "Sir, if I may—I understood that you made certain promises to the Chinese and the rest. Assurances were offered and accepted."

"So they were," Reed told him, smiling. "I'd have promised them the moon and stars to win my country back. Of course, some plans we've made may still proceed. I like the new casino models very much. We could be fabulously rich within a year."

"Yes, sir."

"But they must not forget who holds the real power on Isla de Victoria. I will be president for life, Merrill—and I intend to live a long, long time."

"God willing, sir."

Reed's smile broadened. "We have an understanding, God and I."

Harris was briefly at a loss for words. He settled for, "I'm glad to hear it, sir."

"You think I'm mad, perhaps?"

"No, sir!"

"I wouldn't blame you, Merrill. When the Lord first spoke to me, I thought I'd lost my mind for certain. It was not the sort of information freely shared. It took some time to realize that I am chosen. Blessed."

"Blessed, sir?"

"*Selected,* then, if you prefer. I have a mission to redeem our homeland, Merrill, and to reap the glory from that great achievement."

He couldn't tell if Harris was convinced or not, but Reed's aide-de-camp never forgot his place in the food chain. "I hope I'll be permitted to assist you, sir," he simpered.

"You may begin by doing what I've asked you, Merrill. Carry word to our loyal soldiers. Tell them to be ready if I need to call on them in haste. Remind them who commands the VLM."

"Yes, sir! But Tripp—"

"Will be distracted very soon, I think. There is an inquisition coming. He may not survive it."

"Sir, I don't—"

"It's not important, Merrill. Watch and wait. When Tripp is summoned here, then go and carry out my order."

"Yes, sir!"

"Leave me now."

Reed watched the smaller, darker man retreat. He had chosen Sun's spacious, elaborate garden as the one place where they were least likely to be overheard by eavesdroppers or microphones. The order couldn't wait, after his recent talk with Sun Zu-Wang, and Reed felt better now that he had passed his order on.

The bit about his chats with God had startled Harris, but it had been time to let him know. If he was going to help Reed rule Isla de Victoria, Harris needed to know where his president found inspiration. And if that knowledge ultimately proved too much for him, he could be weeded out, replaced with someone more durable. Someone with faith.

It wouldn't be an easy task, but God provided for his chosen ones. If Reed was forced to jettison his longtime aide and friend, the Lord would find him a replacement he could trust.

Meanwhile, he would trust Harris until circumstances demonstrated that his trust had been misplaced.

And if that happened, Harris wouldn't need to fear the Lord Almighty.

He would get a taste of Hell on Earth.

"INCREDIBLE!" SEMYON Borodin threw up his hands in a theatrical show of amazement. "How many men dead now? Fifty? One hundred?"

Nicolai Yurochka took the cue and said, "No telling. Who can trust the news we get?"

The lean Colombian, Pablo Aznar, sipped a glass of Scotch whiskey and said, "It is cause for concern, there's no doubt."

"Concern, he says." Borodin rolled his eyes and slapped Yurochka's meaty bicep. "I'd say it's a cause for more than that! Who knows which one of us will be the next to go?"

Kenji Tanaka, two days off the plane from Tokyo, exhaled a stream of gray cigar smoke, scanning faces from behind the mirrored sunglasses he wore despite the fact that they were gathered in a dimly lighted dining room. "So much for criticism," he declared. "What would you have us do that is not being done already?"

"That's the point, now, isn't it?" said Borodin. He knew how to play an audience of rough men like himself. It was a talent—like the gift for knowing when to shut his mouth and strike—that had allowed him to survive this long. "The truth is, we don't know what's being done."

"You don't trust Sun Zu-Wang?" Tanaka asked.

Borodin knew he was on thin ice now. The Asians sometimes stuck together, even if their histories were rife with conflict spanning generations. Japanese and Chinese had been at each other's throats from time immemorial, but let a white man challenge any Asian in their presence, and the blood won out.

"I didn't say that, did I?" Borodin replied. "All I've said is that with so much secrecy in place, we don't know what is happening. First, we hear that the Italians in America are being killed like flies. Now it's the Chinese dying, in our own backyard."

"Not *your* backyard," Aznar corrected him.

"A figure of speech, if you please! We're all partners in this enterprise, are we not?"

"Partners, *da*," Yurochka echoed.

"Equal partners," Tanaka inserted. "No masters."

"Exactly!" Borodin flashed a predatory smile and shifted in his seat, making room for the Belgian FN Five-seveN autoloader wedged into the waistband of his tailored slacks. It was uncomfortable, gouging his back, but he still felt better with its twenty rounds of ammunition behind him, even in a "friendly" gathering of thieves and killers.

"*Equal* partners," Borodin repeated, craning toward Tanaka. "Meaning that we should be briefed on everything that happens *when* it happens, not kept in the dark like a pack of poor relations."

"Sun's report seemed straightforward to me," said Tanaka. "He told us what happened and described the action taken to correct the situation."

"If it's not too late," Borodin suggested.

"Too late," Yurochka parroted, then turned away when Borodin pinned him with a glare.

"Why are you worried?" Aznar challenged. "You've lost nothing."

"What better time to worry?" Borodin retorted. "Will it do me any good when I've lost everything?"

"If you're afraid, why not pull out?" It was Tanaka's turn to smile. "We have enough money between us. You can take yours back and *dah svedanya*."

"You misunderstand me," Borodin answered. "I seek no release from my promise, merely some assurance that our enterprise has not gone astray. If we're at mortal risk, why not admit it? All of us are worldly men. We've all spilled blood to reach our present lot in life."

"Some more than others," Aznar ventured.

"As you say. But none of us are virgins, eh? We don't run off like women at the sound of gunfire. If we're truly partners in this undertaking, we should share in the decision-making process."

"And the risks?" Tanaka challenged.

"Yes! Of course! I welcome them."

"I'm glad to hear it," said a voice behind him, almost at his shoulder. Borodin turned in his chair to find Sun Zu-Wang at his back. The man's smile encompassed all present, but it seemed to hold an extra hint of ice for Borodin.

"There are decisions to be made," Sun said, "and one at least that cannot wait. I've summoned Tripp to brief us on security precautions and to find out what went wrong last night. If we determine that his answers are not satisfactory, it may be necessary to replace him."

Borodin knew what that meant. The security chief on a project like theirs was not simply dismissed if he failed in his duties. An example would be made of Tripp, if they decided he must go.

And who would take his place?

"When do we vote?" Borodin asked.

"Tripp's on his way to join us as we speak," Sun answered. "He'll be here within the hour, to plead his case. You are the jury, gentlemen. I trust you'll hear him out and render a decision worthy of your wisdom and experience."

"Of course we will," said Borodin before any of his companions had a chance to speak. "The poor bastard deserves no less!"

SO, HERE WE GO AGAIN, thought Garrett Wesley Tripp.

It wasn't the first time he'd found himself in deep shit, but it was potentially the most dangerous showdown of his life. That fact was all the more ironic, Tripp considered, since he was compelled to face his adversaries empty-handed and alone.

No sweat, he told himself. Just lay things out the way they are. Talk straight. Put the responsibility where it belongs and let them know you're still the best man for the job.

All that could be a problem, though, if one or more of his inquisitors prejudged the case. For all he knew, Tripp could be on his way to face a firing squad, rather than a board of inquiry.

His judges were tough bastards, each and every one of them. Whether they were Russian, Chinese, Japanese, Colombian or Sicilian, each was a certified killer with hundreds of soldiers behind him. Tripp would match his jungle fighting and survival skills against any one of them on demand, any day of the week, but he wasn't fool enough to think he could defy the whole damned crew and walk away from it.

Not in this life.

Which meant that he would have to plead his case persuasively and sway enough votes on the board to keep himself alive.

One of the Chinese hardmen came to fetch him, moving with an almost feline grace that marked him as a likely martial artist. Tripp wasn't sure what it would take to put him down, bare-handed, but he knew he'd never get the chance. If this was his last day on earth, the shooters were already waiting for him, tucked away somewhere behind the scenes.

"This way, sir, if you please."

Tripp followed his guide to the conference room and entered to find the gang all present, minus one. A speaker phone sat in front of an empty chair on his left, no sign of Dante Ambrosio in the flesh. His other judges were assembled, though: Aznar, Tanaka, Sun and Borodin, each representing a faction of the syndicate that had bankrolled Maxwell Reed's campaign to seize control of Isla de Victoria.

If Tripp had a certified enemy in the room, he knew it would be Borodin. The Russian had argued against hiring mercs to direct the guerrilla campaign, angling for a decisive piece of the action himself, but he'd gone along reluctantly when the others hired Tripp. A thumbs-down vote would vindicate him now and put Borodin in position to seize effective control of the show—assuming he could pull it off.

Not yet, Tripp thought. I'm not dead yet.

"Be seated, please," said Sun Zu-Wang, directing Tripp to a chair strategically positioned in front of the conference table.

Tripp sat and waited for the grilling to begin.

It was Sun's territory, his task to start the ball rolling, and he wasted no time. "What can you tell us of the recent attacks, Mr. Tripp?" Sun inquired.

"Nothing, so far," Tripp said. "My people weren't assigned to watch the target, as you know. It was a Triad operation, unrelated to my mission. I've dispatched a team to question the survivors, but their stories don't add up to much. Searching the forest is a waste of time and manpower. Those who got closest to the enemy are dead."

"What *can* you tell us?" asked Tanaka.

"From the evidence, I'd say the raiders were professional, well-trained, well-armed. It was a small team, but I can't quote any numbers."

"Small?" the Russian interrupted him. "Why small, pray tell?"

"Because they ran from mediocre reinforcements, Mr. Borodin. Because they left survivors at the plant. A large force would've shot down the choppers and leveled the compound."

"But they killed their pursuers in the jungle," Borodin reminded him.

Tripp nodded. "That was skill, not superior force. One man can kill a hundred if he's left to pick the time and place."

A hiss of static from the speaker phone gave way to Dante

Ambrosio's thickly accented voice. "Is this attack related to the trouble in Miami and New Orleans?" he demanded.

"Once again, with all respect," Tripp said, "I can't be positive, but I've never put much faith in coincidence. I'll assume a connection and work from that premise until I'm proved wrong, unless Mr. Sun has something to tell us…?"

"Nothing," Sun replied stiffly, while the others swiveled in their chairs to watch him. "If I knew who was responsible, they would have been eliminated."

"I expected no less," Tripp said, letting his judge off the hook. "We need to treat these incidents as related until they're proven otherwise."

"Which brings us back to you, I think," Borodin remarked. "You failed to stop these people in America, when you had the chance. Now, here they are, upsetting everything."

"Again, with all respect," Tripp said, "one drug plant isn't everything. In fact, it plays no part at all in our campaign for Isla de Victoria."

Sun's narrowed eyes regarded Tripp with frank suspicion, but he didn't challenge the assertion. Rather, he interjected, "Tell us, then, if you would be so kind, how you intend to put it right."

"Of course," Tripp said.

They listened, then excused Tripp while they huddled to debate his plan. Kenji Tanaka recognized a gamble when he saw one, and he waited to hear what the others would say before he committed himself.

Predictably the Russian spoke before their host. "I give him points for nerve," said Borodin, "but honestly! Can he believe this scheme will possibly succeed?"

"He's bet his life on it," Pablo Aznar replied. "I can't imagine he would risk so much unless he thought there was a chance."

"With all respect," the Russian answered back, "that's pure bullshit!"

Tanaka watched the slim Colombian lean forward in his chair, hands pressed flat on the tabletop. His dark eyes skewered Borodin as he replied, "Is that what Russians call respect?"

"Don't take offense, my friend." Borodin's smile was a study in calculated mockery. "We're men of the world who speak plainly, yes? You know as well as I do that Tripp is on trial for his life. He's failed us—what? Three times?"

"I don't count this against him," interjected Sun Zu-Wang. "He's right to say his people were excluded from defensive preparations at the plant. If there was fault in this, it lies with me."

"The choice was yours," said Borodin. "You bear the loss. Say that he's only failed us twice, then, with the losses in America. Still, he should be eliminated and replaced."

"Replaced by whom?" Tanaka asked the room at large.

"I have connections," Borodin replied. "In Russia there are many military personnel superior to Tripp's gang of mercenaries. We have former Spetznaz, KGB —"

"We all have friends in uniform," Aznar interrupted. "Come to that, Panama was once part of my country, before the Americans stole it away to build their canal."

"That's ancient history," said Borodin.

"And we are deviating from the proper subject of discussion," Sun reminded all of them at once. "Before replacements are selected, we must first decide if Mr. Tripp still represents us—and if not, what should be done with him."

"He knows too much to let him walk away," the Russian offered.

Sun nodded, conceding the point. "Let us vote, then, on his plan."

"Too risky!" Borodin declared. "We've come too far and paid out too much cash to throw it all away like this."

"It's only lost," Tanaka countered, "if he fails."

Borodin looked around the room, studying each of his colleagues in turn. "If he fails? *If* he fails?" The Russian feigned amazement. "He's already failed twice! Now he wants to gamble everything on this fantastic plan to—"

"Why fantastic?" Sun inquired, turning to face the Russian squarely.

"Did you listen to him?" Borodin seemed flabbergasted, as if he suddenly found himself surrounded by madmen. "Am I the only one who heard this so-called plan?"

"We heard him," said Tanaka, "but we may not have your stake in seeing Tripp removed."

"So, you forgive him?"

"No," Sun answered. "We will hold him to account. If he does not succeed this time, he pays the price."

"If he does not succeed," said Borodin, "our plans and cash go down the shitter. Last time, we lost our friends in the United States. Now, he wants to put our puppet on the chopping block."

"A calculated risk," Tanaka said.

"And if these phantom soldiers take him out, what then? Where will we find another president for Isla de Victoria?"

Sun shrugged. "The same place we found Maxwell Reed. With money and support, we can promote whichever peasant pleases us."

Borodin shook his head. "I still say—"

"Call the vote!" Dante Ambrosio's disembodied voice demanded from the speaker phone.

"He's right," Sun said. "We're wasting time."

"You know my vote already," Borodin responded. "I'm against it."

"Noted." Sun turned toward the far end of the table and the square box of the speaker phone. "Don Ambrosio?"

"I say try it. Kill him if it fails."

"One vote for each side, then. Señor Aznar?"

"Do it," said the Colombian, still eyeing Borodin with thinly veiled contempt.

"Two votes in favor. Mr. Tanaka?"

The Yakuza boss nodded slowly. "Give him the rope. He'll either snare our enemies or hang himself."

"Three votes in favor—and I cast my vote with the majority," Sun said. He turned again to Borodin. "Of course, you are free to disagree."

"And lose my investment by leaving? No, thank you. But mark my words, one and all. When Tripp fails again, you'll see that I was right!"

"And if that happens, we shall vote again," Sun said. "For now, however, it's resolved. I'll deliver the verdict and finalize arrangements to put the plan in motion. Gentlemen, good day."

CHIANG KAI-SHIN CRAVED a cigarette, but he dared not light one without Sun's permission and it would be a show of weakness to ask. Instead he focused on Tripp's face and listened as the master of his family pronounced the mercenary's fate.

"We have agreed to try your way," Sun said, "but there are grave concerns regarding a potential failure."

Tripp nodded his understanding. "As I said, sir—"

"Don't speak yet," Sun interrupted him. "I've managed to secure a reprieve, but it would be a serious mistake for you to count this as a victory. We need results, and quickly, to resolve this situation in our favor. Do you understand?"

"I do."

"Your plan for using Maxwell Reed as bait strikes some as perilous."

"I don't deny the risk, sir."

"Risks for all concerned, if you should fail," Sun said.

"It's clear to me these shooters followed Reed from Florida to Panama. I don't know how they tracked him," Tripp went on, "but here they are. Smart money says they won't be satisfied until they get a clear shot at the prize. That's when I'll move and scoop them up."

"And should you fail…" Sun left the sentence hanging, but the message was clear.

"I trust you'll take whatever action's necessary to resolve the situation, sir," Tripp said.

Chiang gave him credit for bravado, wondering if he would bear such news as well. If he were tested—

"You've received this final chance because the latest failure was not yours," Sun said. "Perhaps, if I had used your men instead of Chiang's to guard the plant, our adversaries would be dead by now."

Tripp flicked a glance at Chiang and said, "We'll never know, sir. None of us can change the past."

Fair words, but they did nothing to untie the knot in Chiang's stomach. Somehow, he kept his face impassive, understanding that his fate was linked with Tripp's now, in Sun's mind. The two of them would stand or fall together.

"You have the men and the equipment you require?" Sun asked.

"I have enough men for the job, yes, sir. The hardware's not a problem. Given any chance at all, I'm hoping to take one or two of them alive and find out who they're working for."

"I won't delay you any longer, then," Sun told the mercenary. Tripp rose from his chair, showed his respect by bowing slightly from the waist, and took his leave. The door closing behind him had a sound of grim finality.

"The Russian had a point, you know," Sun said when they were left alone.

"A point, sir?"

"It's a mighty risk we're taking, Chiang. Reed is the figurehead of the Victorian Liberation Movement. If we lose him now…"

"You said that he could be replaced."

"Of course, with time and effort. Anyone can be replaced, Chiang. You'd do well to keep that fact in mind."

"Sir, I—"

"A wise man knows when silence serves him best. The plant was no great loss, I grant you. But the drugs, the men, and the embarrassment—I cannot tolerate another failure on that scale. You understand?"

"Yes, sir."

"I shall expect you to cooperate with Tripp in every way possible. Should he fail, it must not be through lack of attention on our part."

"No, sir."

"I cannot and will not allow Borodin to believe that the Triad is weak," Sun continued. "We will show him a united face. A ruthless face, when necessary. If a sacrifice is called for, I will make it without hesitation. Understood?"

Chiang nodded silently. He understood only too well.

If Sun determined that a sacrifice was necessary to preserve the coalition he had helped to organize, Garrett Tripp would not die alone. A demonstration of fortitude would be required to let Sun and the Triad save face. Some of the blood Sun spilled to satisfy that need would be Chinese.

Chiang's blood, in point of fact.

"I trust you not to disappoint me, Chiang," his master said.

"No, sir."

"And if you do— " Sun raised his open hands and brushed the palms together lightly, as if dusting them, then raised both hands to heaven. "Go," he said, "and do what must be done."

Chiang went—and wondered as he left the conference room if there was any way to save himself.

5

The hardware was laid out on Bolan's bed, field stripped and cleaned, awaiting reassembly and reloading. The new guns seemed in perfect working order, no apparent defects in their firing pins, actions or magazines. Loading the mags was busy work. It gave them time to talk about their plan, such as it was.

"When do we start this razzle-dazzle business?" Keely Ross inquired of no one in particular.

"Sundown," Bolan answered. "We'll be starting with the local Triad bosses, hoping to shake something loose."

Like Maxwell Reed.

His companions didn't need to be reminded of the puzzle's missing piece. Reed was the key to any action they might undertake—or one of them, at least—and so far Bolan didn't have a clue where he was hiding. Still, the situation wasn't hopeless.

Not yet.

Bolan picked up the H&K PSG-1 sniper rifle, using a hand towel to clean off a shiny patina of oil. Mechanically, the weapon was identical to Heckler and Koch's G-3 assault rifle, introduced four decades earlier, except that it was limited to semiautomatic fire. A 6 x 42 telescopic sight with illuminated crosshairs was an integral part of the rifle. The PSG's bolt was specially engineered to permit silent closure, while an adjustable shoe provided a variable-width trigger with a three-pound pull. The length of stock, drop of butt and height of cheekpiece were also adjustable, while a supporting bipod provided extra stability. Once target acquisition was achieved, the PSG-1 could hurl its projectiles downrange at a muzzle velocity of 2,850 feet per second.

Nothing made of flesh and blood could stand against that shocking force—but Bolan had to find his target before he could bring it down.

And he had an idea of where to start looking.

"Sun Zu-Wang or Chiang Kai-shin?" Johnny asked.

"Make it Sun," Bolan answered. "We may as well start at the top."

They had received a briefing on the local players from Hal Brognola and the intelligence team at Stony Man Farm before embarking on the flight to Panama. Numerous syndicates had fingers plunged knuckle-deep into the local pie, dealing primarily in arms and drugs, but the Chinese Triads were presently on top of the heap—and Sun Zu-Wang's White Lotus Triad Society was the dominant mob in the country. Brognola's techies had tracked White Lotus contributions to Maxwell Reed and the Victorian Liberation Movement through a maze of banks and paper corporations, back to Sun's doorstep in Panama City. If Sun didn't know where the would-be president of Isla de Victoria was hiding, he could find out in minutes by pulling the requisite strings.

But he would require persuasion.

Bolan had played that game before.

"You want to try for him at home?" Grimaldi asked. The pilot's nimble hands were reassembling one of the Spectre submachine guns, as deft with killing hardware as they were at the controls of a flying machine.

"It makes more sense than the office downtown," Bolan replied. "Fewer civilians, more lag time before we run into the heat. If we're lucky, we might even find Reed hanging around the old homestead."

"We may find an army guarding that homestead," Grimaldi countered.

He was right, of course. Sun's home-away-from-Hong Kong was a ninety-acre walled estate on the northern outskirts of Panama City. The wall in question was topped by razor wire and averaged ten feet in height. Inside the wall, Sun's high-tech mansion stood beside a manmade lake, surrounded by a forest of imported trees and shrubs. Aerial photos displayed the layout, but Bolan couldn't be clear on all the security measures until he hit the ground running and took it from there.

"So, what's the master plan?" asked Ross. "Are we ringing the doorbell or going over the wall?"

"I was thinking we might drop in from the air," Bolan said.

Grimaldi's lean face lit up with a smile. "Now you're talking. I can have the chopper airborne with thirty minutes' notice to the airport tower. After the insertion, there's a few tricks I can try to keep the ground team off your backs until you're ready for them."

"Play that part of it by ear," Bolan suggested. "When we're done, I'd rather have a ride home than a fireworks show."

"Amen to that!" Ross added, frowning at the notion of an air drop into Sun's estate.

"No sweat," Grimaldi promised. "With a little work, I can put them through the original Chinese fire drill."

"As long as we're not the ones who go down in flames," Johnny said with a lopsided smile.

"Hey, kid, I haven't dropped you yet."

"Let's hope there's no first time," Johnny replied.

"Grimaldi Airlines aims to please." He turned to Bolan, sitting with the Spectre in his lap and a 50-round mag in one hand. "It's forty minutes to the airport, give or take. Call it an hour and a quarter to liftoff from the time we leave."

"We'll go at seven," Bolan said. "Figure to hit the deck by nine o'clock."

Four hours and change by his watch, before they were back in the eye of the storm.

Washington, D.C.

"I'M GLAD YOU COULD make it, Mr. Koontz."

"No problem. And call me Avery, please."

Hal Brognola moved around with hand outstretched to meet his visitor. Avery Koontz was a red-faced man with thinning hair and the makings of middle-age spread at his waist. Brognola smelled a hint of liquor on the man's breath and nearly checked his watch to verify that it was only 2:30 p.m.

When they had settled into their respective chairs, the desk between them, Brognola said, "We may as well get down to business, then."

"You've got me curious, all right," Koontz answered. "I can tell you, it surprised me to find out you work for Justice."

"Oh? Why's that?"

"Hey, think about it." Koontz was working on a smile that stopped short of his eyes and failed to convey any serious mirth. "A thing like this, I'd have expected someone from the Pentagon or Langley, maybe State. But Justice? That's a new one."

Brognola affected a casual air. "These days, you know, we all do what we can."

"But overseas? This kind of paramilitary action? That sounds like a stretch."

"You'd have to take that up with the Attorney General or the President," Brognola said.

Koontz frowned and raised an open hand, as if he were directing traffic. "No offense, there, Hal. You don't mind if I call you Hal?"

"Suits me, Avery." Brognola could think of other things to call his guest, but at the moment he was looking for cooperation. "Getting back to this joint operation—"

"I have to stop you there," Koontz interrupted him.

"Because?"

"Because there's no joint operation, Hal."

"I guess you'd better tell me what that means, Ave."

Koontz didn't quite flinch at Brognola's tone, but it made him squirm a little in his chair. "I would've thought you knew already," he replied. "Some kind of failure to communicate, I guess."

"Why don't you fill me in?"

"Can do. We kicked the plan around at DHS and came to a decision that our mandate doesn't cover chasing people in and out of other countries. It was a bit too far afield from the concept of homeland defense for the secretary's taste. Someone should have told you."

Someone had, but Brognola wanted to hear it from the horse's mouth—or some other part of the equine anatomy. Angry but not surprised, he studied Koontz as if the red-faced man had just crawled out from underneath a rotting log.

"You're telling me you've got an agent in the field and you've cut off support?" he asked.

"No way," Koontz promptly answered. "If we'd put an agent in the field, there'd be support. Our former agent was advised of the department's policy and ordered to refrain from any further involvement in the campaign. When she fought us on that, we parted company. Simple."

Unless you like to sleep at night, Brognola thought. But what he said was, "So, you're really in the dark about what's going on?"

"I wouldn't say—"

"In terms of national security, I mean."

"Our mandate at the DHS is to protect America," Koontz answered, extra color rising in his florid cheeks.

"Which you propose to do by standing at the border, watching for invaders?"

"I came over here to see you as a courtesy," Koontz said stiffly. "If you want to argue policy, you're wasting everybody's time. I simply carry out the orders I receive."

"Where have I heard that line before?" Brognola asked.

"We're finished here." Koontz rose as he spoke, taking time to straighten his jacket. "Any complaints should be addressed to the undersecretary's office."

"That's one way to go," Brognola replied.

"Meaning what, exactly?"

"Meaning that you're right. We're finished here."

Koontz huffed his way out of the office, closing the door with more force than it needed to get the job done. Brognola dismissed him. By the time Koontz reached the elevator, Stony Man Farm was on the line and Brognola was patched through to the officer in charge of research.

"Panama?" the voice came back at him. "I'd try the embassy first, sir."

"I need someone specific," said Brognola.

"Right. In that case, sir, if you can hold for thirty seconds—"

"Try fifteen."

"Yes, sir."

The man was back in ten with the name. Brognola smiled and said, "Reach out to him, ASAP. Tell him he should expect a call."

"Yes, sir!"

One down, Brognola thought as he replaced the telephone receiver in its cradle. Now all he had to do was reach out to Mack Bolan and pass on the word for a meet in the middle of God-only-knew what kind of action might be going on.

"No sweat," he told himself.

And thought, Just blood.

Panama City

"PENNY FOR YOUR THOUGHTS," Johnny said.

Keely Ross glanced up from the English-language news-paper she'd been skimming and smiled wearily. "You wouldn't get your money's worth."

"Worried?"

"Worn out would be more like it. How the hell do you keep up this pace?"

"I don't, most of the time," he told her honestly. Fudging a bit, he added, "This is a bit unusual for me, as well."

"A bit?"

"Well—"

"What you mean to say is that you've done this kind of thing before and walked away from it."

"That's true," he said, "although it's never quite the same from one time to the next."

"Still, that's a hopeful sign, right?" Ross folded the paper and laid it aside. "I mean, because you're still alive and all."

"So far."

Johnny was loading guns and magazines into a duffel bag. He fought the urge to let it go and join her on the bed.

"Okay, I'll trust your judgment, then," Ross said. "But where on Earth did you find your friends?"

"They're not so different from anybody else," he answered.

"Ri-i-ight. And I'm the Playmate of the Year."

You could be, Johnny almost said, but caught himself in time. "They've been around," he said. "That's all. They've had some training, seen some action. Made some choices in the process."

"That's an understatement."

"They've got some moves, I'll grant you that."

"I'd hate to have them on the other side."

"No fear of that," he told her with complete assurance.

"If I had my druthers, though," she said, "I'd stick with you."

"Hey, flattery will get you anywhere," he answered.

"Will it, really?"

Johnny wasn't sure where she was going with the line of conversation, but it made him nervous. All the more because it felt so right. He changed the subject, asking her, "What will you do when this is finished?"

She watched him for a long, silent moment, seeming vaguely disappointed, before she answered, "You mean job-wise?"

Johnny nodded.

"I haven't really thought about it."

"I just wondered if the door was really closed at DHS."

"I've closed the door on them," Ross said. "I didn't sign on for the political nonsense, you know?"

"I guess it comes with the territory."

"That's why I'm branching out," she told him with a smile. "New territory, new players."

"And how do you like it so far?"

Ross met his level gaze, not smiling now. "It takes some getting used to, but it has benefits."

They were alone in the hotel room. Bolan had retired to his own room for some sleep and Grimaldi was off studying city maps and charted flight paths from the local airport to their target. Johnny felt the heat between himself and Ross as if the air-conditioning in their room had been replaced by a furnace turned up full-blast.

"We have time," she said, as if reading his thoughts.

"Time's not the problem," Johnny answered.

"So, what is?"

"It could mean trouble."

"We have that, already," she replied. "We may as well enjoy it while we have the chance."

"It could get in the way."

"For who? Or is it 'whom'?"

"At some point, you may have to make a choice," he said. "It may be life or death, with no time to debate it. If you get distracted, even for a second, it could be too late."

"I've got my eyes wide open," she assured him as her hands moved to the buttons of her blouse.

"Me, too."

THE MAPS OF PANAMA CITY were fine, as far as they went. Grimaldi had two spread out on his bed, surrounded by aerial photos of Sun Zu-Wang's estate. As usual, the worst part wouldn't be approaching the LZ. He'd file a phony flight plan with the tower, tell them he was taking customers upstairs to see the city lights, and then he'd work around to Sun's place on a route that didn't send up any flags.

Finding the target was no problem.

The trick was inserting Bolan's team and lifting off again before somebody on the ground got wise and started cranking off rounds, maybe sent up a stinger to blow his ass out of the sky. Military hardware was the Triad's stock in trade—well, one of them, at least—and Grimaldi had no illusions about the risk of tackling a Triad chief in his own backyard. Sun could be as well protected as the President of the United States— but that didn't mean he was safe from the Executioner.

After inserting the team, Grimaldi's job was relatively simple. All he had to do was hang around the general neighborhood and pick them up on Bolan's signal, assuming that it ever came. And if it didn't, if the worst-case scenario was finally realized—well, Grimaldi knew damned well he'd try to make the pickup anyway. He owed Bolan that much, for old time's sake.

He owed it to himself.

Ideally, he would've preferred to go in with a fully armed gunship and level Sun's palace with rockets or "smart" bombs, maybe pick off the stragglers with a 2 mm Gatling gun from a hundred yards out. That would get the job done, but it wouldn't help Bolan obtain the combat intelligence he needed to pursue the rest of his mission.

So he studied the maps and the photos, deciding on an approach from the north that would bring him in behind the manor house, skimming treetops on the side of the estate where cover was most plentiful. Bolan's team could rappel from the chopper on static lines with quick-release clips to unleash on touchdown. It was dicey, but better than landing the bird on Sun's driveway to let them step out onto concrete, with every shooter in the compound waiting to receive them.

A gamble either way, but he was used to taking chances with his life—and with those of his friends.

That didn't make it any easier, of course.

Grimaldi wasn't sure exactly how things worked in Panama, what kind of money was available, but he suspected the cops might have a chopper or two in their arsenal, and he couldn't rule out television eyes in the sky once reports of the action were filed. That meant witnesses, maybe some high-flying gunplay, and it brought him to the issue of their getaway.

Bolan's strike on the rural drug plant was one thing, removed from any major urban area, convenient for in-and-out flying without witnesses. An urban strike was something else entirely, meaning that Grimaldi couldn't go back to the airport afterward. It would invite suspicion, at the very least, and if their chopper was identified, it meant a surefire kiss of death.

That was why Grimaldi had a backup plan in place.

His fallback LZ was a small private airstrip east of the city that catered to charters and sight-seeing flights. From the look of the place, Grimaldi suspected a fair amount of contraband had also passed across its runways—a suspicion confirmed when the proprietor questioned nothing but the size of Grimaldi's nonrefundable cash deposit. A berth would be waiting for them, if and when they needed it, but even that would be a stopgap measure if police or Triad soldiers pursued them.

In that event, the best course of action would be to leave the country post-haste. But Grimaldi knew Bolan well enough to understand that evacuation was not anywhere in their immediate future.

The big guy would stay until his work was done.

Or until it killed him.

Grimaldi didn't want to see that happen, but he knew it was a possibility. And he'd be hanging in to the end, no matter how bitter that turned out to be.

THE FIRST TIME WAS A BLUR, all flesh and fumbling, nerves and need. The second time was different—not *better*, she decided, but less frantic and more intimate somehow, because they took a bit more time.

Exploring.

Learning one another, inside out.

They had decided to unwind with separate showers, thinking that a joint attempt at cleanliness would likely turn into Round Three and make them late for Zero Hour.

"Wouldn't want to miss the war," she muttered as the shower swept her words away.

In fact, she wouldn't really mind missing it, but she'd come too far, seen and done too much, to simply back out of the game and pretend it was all a mistake. Dropping out was no longer an option, and she wondered if it ever had been.

Ross wondered, too, how much of her problem was simple duty consciousness and how much was Johnny Gray.

He'd been right about the change that came with intimacy,

but she didn't think it was a bad thing. They already watched each other's backs in battle, and it wasn't as if they would be going for a quickie under fire. If she cared more about him now, that simply meant she'd keep a better watch on him when they were catching hell. It didn't mean that Ross would slack off on her duties where the others were concerned or jeopardize their mission.

Would the others know? She wondered.

And would they care, if they did?

She guessed not, as long as neither she nor Johnny let their extracurricular contact get anyone injured or killed. Until that point, she reasoned, it would likely be a matter of "don't ask, don't tell."

She turned the shower off and reached for a towel, startled into yelping when someone handed it to her.

"Johnny?"

"Who else?" he asked her.

"God, I didn't hear you." Too damned busy worrying, she thought but didn't say.

"Sorry," he replied. "I didn't mean to spook you."

"No spooks here," she told him, putting on a smile before she pulled the shower curtain back and stood in front of him, sleek and dripping wet.

"Now that's a picture," Johnny said.

"You'd better make it a Polaroid. We're running out of time."

"You're right." He nodded toward the shower. "My turn?"

"Be my guest."

They brushed against each other, striking sparks, but Ross kept going on sheer force of will, moving back to the bedroom and her scattered clothing. It was time to change, selecting night garb of another sort. This time around, she would be dressing for invisibility, not for allure.

The mission was her priority. The brass in Washington could yank her badge and paycheck, run her benefits and pension through the shredder, but they couldn't touch her soul unless she let them.

And she wasn't letting them.

Not this time.

"That was quick," a voice behind her said.

She turned to find him standing with a towel around his waist, hair plastered flat, shiny from the shower. She was buckling her belt, ready to go. She hadn't heard him turn the water off.

"That's me," she said. "I'm dressed to kill."

"Keely—"

"Don't say it!"

"What?" he asked her, frowning.

"I don't know. Whatever's on your tongue right now, just swallow it, okay? I can't be soft and girly now. We're out of time."

"Okay."

He dropped the towel and started to dress without another word. Ross wasn't sure if she had hurt his feelings or if Johnny understood.

Good men were hard to find.

Hard men were good to find.

And there were times when being *hard* was all about survival, when any kind of tenderness could get a soldier killed.

Times like tonight.

The gear was packed in duffel bags. As Johnny handed one of them to Ross, he flashed a killer smile and said, "Let's go, partner."

GRIMALDI DROVE THE WAY he flew, pushing the envelope whenever possible, but he was smart enough to know they didn't need a traffic stop when they were headed for the airport with an arsenal on board.

"I fixed it with the tower," he told Bolan when they'd traveled two long blocks. "We're good to go, if nothing happens prior to liftoff."

"Don't say that," Ross chided from the back seat. "You'll jinx us."

"I don't believe in jinxes," Grimaldi replied. "We make our own luck as we go along."

Bolan tuned out the banter, watching through his window as they left a residential area behind, cruising past shops and offices, a theater, a stately bank, more offices and shops. When dwellings next appeared they were distinctly downscale, little more than tenements. There were more people on the street, presumably because their homes offered less comfort, less excitement than the seedy world outside.

In his experience, it always worked that way. Airports and factories were built as far away as possible from stylish homes, whose wealthy occupants had no desire to breathe in toxic fumes or hear jet engines howling day and night. Low-income housing was the order of the day in districts zoned for heavy industry and transportation—and sometimes, especially in Third World cities, that translated to *no* housing. Poverty pockets provided cheap labor, people who didn't complain about noise or pollution. Or, if they did, no one listened because they weren't greasing the wheels with cash. Only their low-rent flesh and blood.

He was amazed, sometimes, that residents of slums and ghettos all over the world didn't rebel en masse against the societies that denigrated them. Bolan tried not to think of it often, tried not to dwell on the fact that Injustice was too vast a foe for any lone soldier to tackle in combat. He did what he could, on a one-to-one basis, and carried the rest of the weight on his soul.

Jobs unfinished.

"Okay," Bolan said, interrupting some spiel of Grimaldi's he hadn't been following, "are we all clear on what's happening?"

To their credit, no one groaned out loud. They'd been over it half a dozen times already, plotting their movements with aid from the aerial photos. Bolan trusted his teammates, but he needed to hear it one more time.

"Solid," Grimaldi replied, grinning. "We come in from the north and I hold steady while you do the bungee thing."

Not quite, but close enough. They were rappelling, not leaping from the chopper, but Grimaldi's sense of humor was irrepressible. He knew how much was riding on his skill and timing. He never lost sight of the mission, but he wouldn't let it blind him, either.

"And once we're down?" Bolan half turned to face Ross and Johnny, sitting in back with a yard of dead air in between them.

"Fan out," Johnny said, "and make tracks for the house."

"I've got the motor pool this time," Ross said, referring to Sun Zu-Wang's five-car garage. "No wheels, no getaway."

"Unless they run," Bolan reminded them. He didn't have to add, "Unless they kill us first." The possibility of death was never far from any combat soldier's thoughts, but dwelling on it only increased the potential for fumbling mishaps that could make the fear a self-fulfilling prophecy.

"I'll keep them distracted, at least," Grimaldi said.

That part of the plan had been Grimaldi's idea. As soon as Bolan's team was on the ground—and hopefully before the home team rallied to repel them—Grimaldi would do a low-level fly-by on the house, drawing as many defenders as possible toward the front and away from the intruders. Since they couldn't conceal or silence the chopper, Grimaldi had reasoned, they ought to make the racket work for them, turn it from a giveaway to a diversion.

Maybe it would work—and maybe not.

Either way, they would know soon enough.

"Here we go," Grimaldi announced as they joined the flow

of traffic headed for the airport. "Any minute now. Just play it cool and let me do the talking at the hangar."

Fair enough, thought Bolan. His action, in turn, would be upon them soon enough.

Maybe too soon.

Bolan wasn't psychic, but he could predict the night's outcome. There would be bloodshed, fire and pain. As far as *whose* blood would be spilled, however, Bolan didn't have a clue.

He'd simply have to wait and see.

6

"You understand me, then?" asked Sun Zu-Wang.

"Most certainly," said Chiang Kai-shin. "I've seen to everything."

"I hope so. Tripp is bringing reinforcements to the city, but they won't arrive until midnight. Meanwhile, security is our responsibility—and that means *yours*."

Chiang ducked his head, a sign of acquiescence and respect. "Of course, sir. Nothing will be left to chance."

"It was a close thing with our colleagues," Sun explained. "Especially the Russian pig, Borodin. He would like nothing better than to see us fail and have the others turn to him for reassurance."

"They're not that gullible," Chiang answered. "Not Tanaka, anyway. The Yakuza hate the Russians more than we do."

Sun knew all about the racial and political antagonisms that beset their coalition. He knew, for instance, that while Japanese mobsters despised Russia and Russians, they also had no love for the Chinese. Too many wars, atrocities and broken treaties stood between their peoples to permit anything resembling true friendship or trust.

Sun wondered for the thousandth time if they were embarked on a doomed adventure, but he had come too far, chased the dream too long, to simply admit it was all a costly mistake. Success was still within his reach, if he could just live long enough to close his hand around the big brass ring.

"All right," he said at last. "Tell me what you have done so far."

Chiang smiled, obsequious as ever. "I have doubled the guards outside," he replied, "and reinforced security on all our major investments. In addition, I've—"

Whatever Chiang meant to say, his words were eclipsed by a sudden pounding on the study door.

Scowling, Sun barked an order for the man to enter. It was one of his soldiers, wide-eyed with worry, clutching an automatic rifle to his side.

"What is it?" Sun demanded, angry at the interruption.

"Sir, there is a helicopter—"

And before the man could finish his report, Sun heard the airship overhead. For the sound to be so loud inside his ground-floor study, it must have buzzed the house near rooftop level. In a heartbeat it had moved beyond them, shifting toward the front of the house and lingering there, as if the chopper were landing.

"Sir, if you—"

"Get out there!" Sun commanded, fury sparking in an instant. "No one is expected or allowed to land without permission. No one!"

"Sir—"

"Go do your job!"

The soldier vanished, so frightened that he forgot to close the study door behind him. It made no difference, since Sun did not intend to stay where he was.

He moved to the ornate window seat, polished hardwood beneath a tall window facing his flower garden, and stooped to release a hidden clasp. Lifting the seat, Sun quickly scanned the contents: a Type 56-2 automatic rifle with side-folding stock, a Type 79 submachine gun, a Czech Samopal 61 "Skorpion" machine pistol, and a matched pair of Type 59 semiautomatic pistols.

Sun tucked one of the pistols into his belt and held the other balanced in his palm. "Are you armed?" he asked Chiang.

The reply came back, shamefaced. "No, sir."

"Take this."

Sun handed off the second pistol, then picked up the assault rifle. It had a full 30-round magazine already in place. All Sun had to do was cock the weapon and fire, unfolding the stock if he saw any need for more precise shooting. He hadn't fired one of the Chinese rifles in at least five years, but he had not forgotten how. Once learned, the skills might fall into disuse, but they were not forgotten.

"Take whatever else you want," Sun told his aide. "You may be needing it."

THE INSERTION HAD GONE as well as Bolan could have hoped. There was no snarling in the static lines as they descended, no guards in the immediate vicinity to pick them off in midair. The helicopter noise was thunder in his ears, eliminating any hope that he would hear the shooters coming until the chopper had taken off, but Bolan had anticipated that. He was in motion as soon as his feet touched Earth and the lines were unclipped. He made tracks toward the house with the others close behind him.

Grimaldi roared past them and was gone. Bolan listened for sounds of reaction, hoping that any shooters already headed his way would turn back to follow the chopper.

The first sounds of gunfire were muffled by distance and trees, echoing from somewhere up ahead. The house, Bolan supposed, where Grimaldi would be staging his diversion by now, drawing fire from the home team. Bolan trusted the pilot to stay out of harm's way and to keep the chopper airborne until they called him for liftoff. But there was always the chance that one of the shooters would score a lucky hit and take the bird down.

In which case, they were well and truly screwed.

You never hear the shot that kills you.

Bolan was reminded of that soldier's adage when a bullet sizzled past his face, perhaps six inches to his left. He hadn't seen the muzzle flash, had heard the shot only as he ducked for cover, squeezing off a short reflexive burst from his Steyr AUG. Behind him, the others were dodging, as well, alerted to the danger by Bolan's response on point.

"How many?" Johnny's voice came through Bolan's earpiece.

"I can't tell yet."

He glimpsed the muzzle flashes then, at least two weapons were firing from the shadows, twenty-five or thirty feet in front of him. If they had been more patient, let him get a little closer, either gunman could have dropped him in his tracks.

But they had missed their golden opportunity.

Bolan lined up one of the blinking muzzle flashes in his Steyr's sights and stitched the shadows just above it with a 6 round burst that put the sniper out of action. He was swinging to his right, seeking the second target, when Johnny and Ross beat him to it. They fired together, fanning the brush with a tight cloud of 5.56 mm manglers, and the second gun fell silent.

Bolan didn't wait to see if there were more sentries in hiding. The skirmish with the first two would alert others, perhaps draw some back from the house and away from Grimaldi's sideshow. Bolan wanted to meet the newcomers halfway to try to surprise them, instead of waiting for them to choose the time and place of ambush.

It should work, he thought.

A BULLET CRACKED Grimaldi's windscreen, telling him that it was time to split. He took the Agusta A-109 Hirundo chopper up and out of there, its twin engines straining for altitude and speed.

"Come on," he urged the streamlined metal bird. "Let's do it, baby."

Banking as he climbed, Grimaldi veered off to the west, drawing attention from his enemies in that direction, instead of northward toward Bolan's path of advance. The diversion was useless if he blew it in the final moments and led the troops back to his friends.

Below and behind him, the sentries kept firing, but Grimaldi was soon out of range. He had killed his running lights on the approach and left them off now—another violation, but what did it matter in light of the charges he'd face if arrested?

Once out of touch from the ground, he put the chopper in a wide-loop holding pattern, orbiting Sun's estate beyond the reach of naked eyes or gunsights, still within radio range of the summons he waited to hear. When Bolan called him, he would answer.

In the meantime he would watch and wait, until his friends called out to him and told him it was time to go. He'd stay on point and be there when they needed him.

When it was time to fly or die.

THEY SPLIT UP AS planned, on the final approach, with some three hundred yards left to go. Johnny was disoriented by the darkness and the trees, but he held to his course with assistance from lights in the distance, his first glimpse of Sun Zu-Wang's home from ground level.

The firing from that direction had tapered off, then sputtered out, before Johnny realized he could no longer hear the helicopter. Since there'd been no crash, he knew Grimaldi had made it clear and would be circling now, waiting for the call to tell him it was bye-bye time.

He couldn't see Keely Ross, but Johnny's thoughts went out to her. Enough of them, at least, to hope that she was swift and sure in what she had to do, and that she'd come through all of it intact.

Stay focused, he warned himself.

Tonight his mind had to be fully occupied with wet work of another kind.

Even alert, he almost missed the sentries coming for him through the trees. They wore some kind of camouflage, not unlike Johnny's, but their haste betrayed them. Homing on the earlier reports of gunfire, playing catch-up in the dark, they couldn't mask the noise their stumbling progress made.

Johnny slowed, then stopped, crouching behind a stout old tree and sighting down the barrel of his AUG. He reckoned there were at least three shooters. But he knew there might be others coat-tailing the point men, their progress covered by the noise of the others. Still, if he wanted to survive the night, he couldn't wait to verify the head count.

And he most definitely wanted to survive.

Hunched shadows were coming for him, weapons glinting in the filtered moonlight. Johnny tracked from right to left, taking the nearest of them first, then moving on. He milked the AUG for 3- and 4-round automatic bursts, trusting his skill and instinct rather than sticking too long with any one target.

It was more or less like shooting skeet—except these clay pigeons were willing and able to kill.

He might've heard the first one fall, grunting a cry of shock and pain, but Johnny wasn't sure. The AUG's reports were ringing in his right ear, while the earpiece of his headset plugged the left.

He pivoted and fired again. A second shadow buckled, lurched and fell. The third marked Johnny's muzzle flash and was returning fire with a Kalashnikov's distinctive bark. Surprise saved Johnny, as the first rounds came in high and wide, at least three feet above his head and six or eight feet to his left.

Johnny returned fire with interest, chopping his last target down in a flurry of bullets that left the field clear. He waited for a moment, just in case the night held more surprises, then sprang up and moved on toward the house.

"You there, kid?" his brother asked through the tiny earpiece.

"Affirmative," he answered, through the stalk of his voice-activated microphone.

There was no further comment from his brother; he'd expected none. There wasn't time to chat while they advanced on Sun's fortress.

The house loomed large ahead of him as Johnny rushed on through the night and dappled moonlight, toward the killing ground.

THE OTHERS WERE READY and waiting when Sun Zu-Wang went to collect them. Semyon Borodin began barking questions, then lapsed into sullen silence at sight of the weapons Sun and Chiang carried. Pablo Aznar seemed fairly relaxed, as if his nights often included gunfire and the sounds of helicopters swooping overhead. As for Kenji Tanaka and his aide, Tomichi Kano, Sun read nothing on their stern, impassive faces.

Triad guards had led Sun's guests to the conference room, where hours earlier they'd voted more or less unanimously to give Garrett Tripp one final chance. Ironically, the peril they'd been seeking to avoid had overtaken them before Tripp had had an opportunity to put his troops in place.

"It appears we have some difficulty," Sun informed his partners.

"Difficulty?" Borodin replied. "It sounds like war!"

"In any case, you'll find I am prepared. We're leaving now.

A refuge waits. My men will handle this unpleasantness and let us know when it's safe to return."

"Your men, not Tripp's?" the Russian challenged.

"As you understood this afternoon, Comrade, Tripp's reinforcements are en route to Panama by air. He made it clear that they would not arrive before midnight."

"Still, I don't see—"

Sun interrupted Borodin. "I promise you that no one shall be forced to leave against his will. If you prefer to stay and see this through, I'll happily instruct my men to follow any of your orders as they would my own."

Borodin's ruddy face appeared to lose a shade or two of color. "No, no," he answered hastily. "I meant no insult to your leadership, of course."

"None taken." Sun relaxed his index finger slightly on the trigger of his automatic rifle. "In that case, if all of you would follow me."

He led them from the conference room to a service entrance near the southeast corner of the house that led to the way outside.

A concrete helipad was situated thirty yards away. An Aerospatiale Dauphin II helicopter waited for them on the pad, two men at the controls, with seating for eleven passengers. The rotors were already turning lazily, picking up speed as Sun and his party appeared on the lawn.

"We're flying?" asked Tanaka.

"It's faster and safer than driving," Sun replied. "Our enemy may have the driveway under guard."

"But with an aircraft part of the attack—"

"My men drove it away. If it were armed, the pilot would have killed them and we'd all be under fire by now."

"I still think—"

"We should trust our host this far, I think," said Aznar from the sidelines. "And we're wasting time."

Tanaka frowned but dipped his head in a conciliatory gesture. "As you say."

Sun kept his eyes trained to the north as he led the others toward the helicopter. On the flank, his men had formed a skirmish line to deal with any opposition that might surface in the next few moments. After that, it wouldn't matter. They'd be safely on their way.

Reaching the chopper, Sun stood back and let the others enter first, choosing their seats. When Chiang approached the open bay, however, Sun stood in his path.

"You're needed here," he said, registering the stunned expression on Chiang's face.

His first lieutenant managed to control his fear and replied, "Yes, sir. As you command."

"You have the phone number," Sun told him. "Use it to report your victory. I trust you will not keep us waiting long."

"No, sir!"

"Until then." Sun dismissed him, climbing into the helicopter's open maw. One of the crewmen closed the sliding door behind him, then returned to the controls while Sun fastened his own seat belt. A moment later the engines revved and the clumsy-looking aircraft rose with surprising delicacy.

Holding the rifle between his knees, stock planted on the chopper's metal floor, Sun watched his estate dwindle from view. His gaze swept the visible skyline, half expecting an attack despite his own reassurance to Tanaka, but no enemy came racing toward them through the air.

We've done it, he thought. We're safe.

But he kept a firm grip on his weapon, just in case.

KEELY ROSS LOBBED an antipersonnel grenade into the five-car garage through a window in the south-facing wall and followed it with another before the first one exploded. She was retreating when the first grenade went off, the second detonation sounding like an echo from Hell. That impression was reinforced as ruptured fuel tanks spilled their contents, gasoline caught and the tanks went up in rapid fire.

The blast and fire brought shooters running, killer moths drawn to the flame. Ross tracked them from the shadows and began to take them down when they were close enough to make it easy work—no handy cover since she'd taken care of the garage. She dropped one, two, three—letting violence numb her senses.

She hit number four on the run, maybe winged him, then ducked as his companion targeted her muzzle flash. She rolled away, hearing bullets fan the air above and behind her, until the roots of a sculpted hedge halted her progress. The shrubbery wouldn't stop bullets, but at least it offered some concealment while she found the last shooter, chased him with automatic fire and sent him sprawling in the firelight.

Ross was about to congratulate herself on wiping out Sun's motor pool when she heard the sounds of a helicopter passing overhead. There'd been no signal for their pilot to return, but maybe—

Glancing up as she rose, Ross saw an unfamiliar chopper rising swiftly over the estate, banking as it gained altitude and started to retreat. She guessed the hired help wouldn't have a whirlybird at their disposal, but the Triad boss could easily afford one.

"No you don't, dammit!"

Ross shouldered the Steyr, focused its optical sight, and fired a long burst at the shrinking airship. Her magazine emptied before the target faded from sight, apparently unscathed.

More gunmen were advancing now on the garage, on her position, firing as they came. Ross ditched the empty magazine, replaced it with a fresh one, and went back to fighting for her life.

GRIMALDI SAW THE helicopter lift off from a distance, rapidly acquiring altitude and flying westward, leaving behind the embattled estate. He guessed that Sun would be among its occupants and wondered whether Maxwell Reed would also be aboard, the man Bolan was searching for, about to slither through his fingers once again.

Grimaldi thought of giving chase. But his own bird wasn't armed, so there was nothing he could do to stop Sun fleeing, short of pulling off a kamikaze-style attack that would've sacrificed his life. He could track the chopper to its destination but the knowledge that his friends might request liftoff stopped him. He couldn't leave them stranded on the killing field.

Cursing, he watched Sun's helicopter slip away and vanish into darkness.

Cursing again, Grimaldi concentrated on the action playing out below him, near the limit of his unassisted vision. The garage was gone, transformed into a funeral pyre, and he could see no vehicle movement anywhere on the estate. From his range, the muzzle flashes looked a bit like twinkling stars, but there was nothing heavenly about their light. He tried to guess which belonged to Bolan, Johnny and the woman, but it was a futile exercise.

They'd call him when they wanted him, unless they were eliminated first. Meanwhile he had another task—to watch the sky and roads approaching Sun's estate, scanning for danger on the ground or in the air.

Grimaldi circled in the chopper.

Watching and waiting.

DESPITE A MOMENT of initial shock, Chiang wasted no time seething over Sun's abandonment. He was subordinate to Sun Zu-Wang in every sense, and his normal duties included supervising the security arrangements for Sun's home and various Triad properties throughout the country. It was only fitting that he should be left to face the enemy—but still, he felt an unaccustomed twinge of fear.

As soon as they could hear his voice above the rising helicopter noise, Chiang started barking orders to the men around him. There were six of them. He ordered three to remain beside him and dispatched the others to gather reinforcements from the grounds at large. If they met enemies along the way and were unable to dispose of them unaided, Chiang instructed them to return to inform him where the hostile targets could be found.

Three gunmen didn't offer much security, as Chiang heard the explosive sounds of battle moving closer by the moment. The garage, with three sports cars, a Lexus and a Lincoln Town Car parked inside, had gone up in a roaring cloud of smoke and flame before Sun's helicopter had cleared the tree line to the west. Chiang didn't care about the cars but the blast meant that raiders had circled the house and were close to enveloping him.

How many? Who were they?

Chiang had no answers to those questions or the others that vied for attention in his mind. He had to focus on the twin goals of survival and defeating an elusive enemy he so far couldn't see. If it became a choice between one outcome or the other, Chiang knew where his duty lay.

Sun would expect no less than total sacrifice.

He would accept no less—and he would mercilessly punish failure. Chiang preferred his chances on the battlefield to facing Sun with news of another defeat.

Standing in the open with his three young bodyguards made him nervous. The pistol in Chiang's hand felt small and useless, like a toy. He moved back toward the house for shelter, his men moving automatically beside him. As they retreated, Chiang scanned around him, watching for enemies.

Despite his vigilance, however, he was startled when his eyes beheld a black-clad figure skulking at the northeast corner of Sun's mansion.

"There!" Chiang told his soldiers, pointing with his free hand while he cocked the pistol. "See him? In the shadows!"

His companions squinted, craning forward, until one of them let out a squawk and raised his submachine gun in preparation for firing. Chiang slapped the muzzle down, cursing.

"He's too far away for that. Go! Try to take him alive!"

The young soldiers exchanged worried looks, then ran off toward the point where the shadow figure had vanished from sight. Chiang jogged along behind them, making no effort to match their swift pace. He suspected the raider would sell his life dearly, and Chiang wanted no part of the action if he could avoid it.

On the other hand, if they could take the intruder alive and make him talk—.

Before the thought was fully formed, gunfire erupted from the corner of the house where Chiang had glimpsed the stranger. Short bursts of automatic fire cut down his three advance men and left them thrashing on the grass.

Chiang whipped his pistol up and forward, squeezing off a shot even before he had acquired the target.

All in vain.

His enemy's weapon belched flame and a short burst of slugs struck Chiang's chest with sledgehammer force. He pitched over backward, the pistol spinning from fingers already gone numb. It should have frightened Chiang, but it didn't.

In fact, he felt nothing at all.

BOLAN STOOD ABOVE THE dying man and recognized his face from the mug shots Brognola had faxed to Miami before their departure to Panama. Chiang Kai-shin was Sun's second in command and heir apparent in the White Lotus Triad Society.

As for Sun…

Bolan had seen the helicopter fleeing and knew what it meant. Sun was a general, not a foot soldier. It had been years since he'd been forced to soil his hands with wet work, and he wouldn't do so now if there was any viable alternative.

Such as leaving Chiang to face the heat, for instance.

And if Sun was gone, he would have taken any resident VIPs along for the ride.

The most Bolan could hope to accomplish now was to whittle Sun's ranks and trash his home, but neither action would advance his ultimate purpose.

If Maxwell Reed had ever been here, they had missed him. If he wasn't here, they'd missed the chance to question Sun and to learn of Reed's whereabouts. Sun's first lieutenant was beyond all conversation now, and Bolan had no reason to believe that any other soldier on the ground possessed the information he required.

Resigned, he spoke into the microphone. "Sun's gone," he told the others. "This is pointless. Fall back to the pickup point, ASAP."

"Roger!" his brother's voice came back.

"I'm on my way," said Keely Ross.

Bolan was moving, too, as he reached down to change the frequency on the compact two-way radio clipped to his web belt. Static whispered to him for an instant, then was gone.

"Flyboy, you there?" he asked Grimaldi.

"Standing by," was the response.

"We're done here, headed for the pickup. Ought to be there in about one-eighty, if it's cool."

"I'll see you there," Grimaldi promised. "Out."

Bolan turned from the dead and ran toward the dark tree line. Behind him, Sun's guards fired at shadows, perhaps at each other. He left them to it, moving toward the small clearing on the eastern perimeter where Grimaldi had agreed to land the chopper to retrieve them.

It was time to leave this killing place and to find out where the prey had gone to hide. The Executioner could only hope that he could track them down before it was too late.

7

Arthur Gladstone had been jumpy ever since he'd received the 2:00 a.m. wakeup call from his boss at the U.S. embassy in Panama City. It wasn't an everyday thing—hell, it wasn't an every *year* thing—and Gladstone knew from the tone of his superior's voice, the cryptic language he'd employed, that a false step on this unexpected task could have serious repercussions for Gladstone's diplomatic career.

Which wasn't saying much right now, stuck here in Panama, but he had hopes for bigger, better things, and Gladstone didn't want to see them dashed before he had a decent chance to make them real.

It wasn't such a hard job, after all. He simply had to make some phone calls, chat up certain people on the graveyard shift, ask certain simple questions and make note of the replies. Then, shortly after sunrise, he was to wait for contact at a downtown intersection and relay the information to an unnamed stranger.

So why was Gladstone sweating as he made the phone calls? Why was there a tremor in his hand as he took notes? One sheet of paper from the notepad, resting on a solid surface just the way he'd been instructed during basic training, so there'd be no ghost impression on the pad.

The spooks referred to it as "tradecraft." Gladstone had regarded it as foolishness when he was sitting in a well-lit classroom in the middle of a sunny afternoon—but it was different, somehow, in the cold hour before sunrise, when he wasn't even sure that he would be alive come breakfast time.

"Of course I will," he muttered, staring at the note before he folded it and put it in his pocket. But the self-assurance had a hollow ring.

Gladstone considered taking the pistol from his desk. He got as far as the study doorway before he decided against it. He'd purchased the gun without telling his superiors and had practiced with it for all of an hour one evening at a private shooting range. Gladstone knew he wouldn't stand a snowball's chance in Hell against an opponent with any real-world experience in combat. The stories of simple men rising to a challenge under deadly pressure were simply that—stories—and they wouldn't even work in Hollywood without Bruce Willis or Arnie Schwarzenegger cast as the "ordinary" heroes.

Leaving the gun where it was, Gladstone left without waking his wife. The meeting place was two blocks east and one block south of his apartment building, possibly selected for his own convenience. Call it fifteen minutes max, on foot. He didn't take the car because there wouldn't be a parking place; Gladstone didn't want to waste the time maneuvering.

The downtown streets were busy, even at this early hour. He found the corner and settled down to the business of killing time. Window-shopping at an office supply store left him too much time to think, so Gladstone shifted to the jeweler's window next door. The prices dismayed him, reminding him of his wife's taste for expensive baubles, and for a moment he nearly forgot his errand.

A voice hailed him from the curb.

"Are you Gladstone?"

He turned from the window to confront a grim-faced

stranger. The new arrival watched Gladstone from the passenger seat of a nondescript sedan. A second man occupied the driver's seat, ignoring him, preoccupied with traffic.

"That depends," Gladstone replied.

"On the weather, I'll bet," said the stranger. "We're expecting rain by noon."

"Unless the skies clear sooner," Gladstone answered, completing the silly code phrase.

"Okay, get in."

Gladstone approached the car, hesitating for two heartbeats before he climbed into the back seat. His door was barely shut before the driver pulled out from the curb, accelerating smoothly into morning traffic.

"You've got something for me," said the passenger.

"I do," Gladstone agreed.

A silent moment passed before the stranger said, "I'm not a dentist, guy. Don't make me pull teeth."

"Sorry." Gladstone didn't like the image that had come to mind. "I checked on Maxwell Reed and Sun... Is it Zu-Wang?"

"It is. What did you find?"

"They left Panama at half-past five this morning, a private charter flight to Nassau."

The stranger swiveled in his seat and locked eyes with Gladstone. "What else?"

"They weren't alone," Gladstone replied. "There were eight other passengers. Three carried Russian passports, three were Japanese, plus two Colombians."

"You have the names?"

"Right here." Gladstone moved slowly, reaching for the folded note. He watched the stranger read it over, maybe twice.

"Anything else?"

"That's it," Gladstone assured him.

"Right. Then we're done."

The sedan pulled over and Gladstone glanced through his

window, discovering that they had boxed the block and returned to the original pickup point. Apprehension vied with relief as he let himself out of the car and stepped onto the sidewalk.

This was when they'd kill him, if they meant to.

Gladstone stood with his eyes closed, fists clenched at his sides, waiting for the gunshot. A full minute passed before he turned to see that the sedan had gone.

Convinced at last that he would live, the diplomat turned toward home to change his suit before he went to the embassy.

BOLAN STARED THROUGH the helicopter's starboard window, scanning blue water as far as the eye could see. Jamaica lay beyond his range of vision, six hundred miles or more to the northeast of their flight path. The Bahamas were four hundred miles further yet. But they weren't headed north at the moment. Rather, Grimaldi was flying them westward, over the gulf and away from Panama City, homing on the next pit stop in Costa Rica.

A Learjet Longhorn 60 waited for them on the ground at Puerto Limón, gassed up and ready to fly. It had been confiscated from a Mexican drug lord eight months earlier and provided with new registration numbers in preparation for future assignments. Bolan didn't know where else the plane had been, having been captured by the DEA, but he knew where it was going.

Nassau.

The trail had lengthened beyond his expectation in the past two weeks, since Johnny's urgent summons had brought Bolan into this latest campaign of his never-ending war. He didn't mind the change of scene, but a disturbing pattern had begun to form, their primary targets repeatedly slipping through the net.

It was time for a change.

They'd abandoned their hardware on takeoff, unwilling to risk a hang-up with Customs in Costa Rica or the Bahamas. There were weapons to be had in Nassau, the same as anywhere else, and Bolan was still flush with cash from the Miami raids.

The Executioner was planning the next phase of his campaign. It felt like starting from scratch, but that wasn't all bad. Nassau authorities weren't expecting a war on their turf. While police in Panama City were playing catch-up, closing the gap between themselves and Bolan's team, he would be opening a new offensive far beyond their reach—and the Bahamian cops would also be starting from scratch. He couldn't rule out some kind of corrupt influence in Nassau—in fact, Bolan expected nothing less—but he doubted that Reed or his sponsors would welcome police intervention at this point. Most likely, they'd try to settle the problem themselves.

And that was perfect for Bolan.

He was ready and willing to meet their best effort, anytime, anywhere.

If only he could get the men in charge to stand and fight. If he could find the men he wanted, there were ways of forcing them to battle—or at least forcing them to reveal themselves.

At this point, it was all he really wanted. One clean shot at Maxwell Reed, and time to mop up those who paid his way.

Bolan would have to run the names past Hal Brognola, but he had a solid hunch as to their pedigree already. Russians, Japanese, Colombians—all traveling with Reed and Sun Zu-Wang, an identified Triad leader. It didn't take a degree in criminal justice to guess that the others represented factions of the Russian Mafia, the Yakuza and the Colombian drug cartels.

Nassau would be no different in the end, but he would have to mark his targets first, acquire new weapons and make sure no innocent civilians were caught in the cross fire. Bolan flatly rejected the concept of "collateral damage" that some military spokesmen had elevated to a propaganda art form. If he couldn't drop his enemies without harming blameless bystanders, the predators would get a pass to fight another day.

But they would not escape.

Washington, D.C.

HAL BROGNOLA TOOK the call at 10:13 a.m. He lifted the receiver on its first ring, ready for it, and spoke as always to the private line.

"Who's that?"

"Just me," the Executioner replied.

Brognola felt relief at hearing Bolan's voice. Stony Man had captured some radio traffic about last night's blow-up in Panama City, and the intervening silence had begun to make Brognola nervous. He got that sour feeling in his stomach every time there was a firefight and Bolan dropped out of contact.

Worried this time might be the last.

"I heard about the party," said Brognola, sounding casual.

"The guests of honor left early," Bolan replied.

"That's too bad. How'd it go with the embassy guy?"

"Well enough. We're playing catch-up, on our way to Nassau."

"Fun and sun," Brognola quipped.

"That's what they say."

"How can I help?" Brognola knew there must be something. Bolan rarely called with simple updates and never for small talk.

"Two things," the warrior said. "I have some names to check, and we'll need a sitrep on the action in Nassau."

Brognola knew the kind of situation report Bolan wanted. Names and connections, who owns whom, the covert ties that bind.

"The sitrep shouldn't be a problem. Let me have the names."

"First, Semyon Borodin." Bolan spelled it. "He's Russian."

"You think?" Brognola smiled. "Who's next."

"Nicolai Yurochka, traveling with Borodin."

"Okay."

"Pablo Aznar, Colombian."

"That rings a bell. I don't remember if he's Medellin or Cali, but it should be easy to find out. Next up?"

"Two Japanese," Bolan replied. "Kenji Tanaka and Tomichi Kano."

"Yakuza?"

"Smells like it, but I need to verify," said Bolan.

"Right. These guys are traveling with Sun?"

"And Reed, plus their bodyguards. It's one big happy family getting the hell out of Dodge."

"I guess they didn't like the heat."

"They need to find another line of work then," Bolan said.

Too late for that, Brognola thought. Once Bolan had a target's number, there was no escape, no vow or promise that could lift the impending sentence of death. The only way his enemies could help themselves would be to eliminate Bolan first.

"I'll get right this in the pipe, ASAP. Where can I reach you?" Brognola asked.

"Use the cell. We're at a Costa Rican pit stop, changing planes, but we'll be out of here in twenty, thirty minutes."

"Roger that. You know it's not all tourist playground, right?"

"I heard a rumor," Bolan answered.

"I just don't want these suckers taking anybody by surprise."

"We're all on the same page," Bolan told him, speaking for Johnny and Ross. "Which reminds me. What's the scoop on DHS?"

"They're playing deaf and dumb," Brognola said. "As far

as the dumb part goes, I'm not sure it's an act. The guy I talked to seems to worry more about his job than his responsibilities."

Brognola kept things moving. "How are you fixed for gear?" he asked.

"Right now, we're naked. I'll go shopping when we hit the beach."

"Need a referral, while I'm at it?"

"Couldn't hurt," Bolan replied.

Brognola was on the verge of saying, "Watch your back," but knew it wasn't necessary. "I'll be talking to you, then," he said.

The line went dead and he dropped the receiver back into its cradle.

Every time Brognola put an agent in the field, he hoped that agent would succeed and return intact. It didn't always work that way, of course. Sometimes the job used up the man or woman sent to do it.

Sometimes it simply could not be done.

And this time?

He would have to wait and see.

That was the worst part of promotion, being desk-bound. In the not-so-old days, Brognola had been a field agent himself— had met Bolan the first time, in fact, while pursuing a common enemy from different angles of attack. In those campaigns, at least, Brognola had been certain he'd done everything within his power to protect his troops and see the good fight won.

These days everything within his power meant sitting in an office, making phone calls, sending e-mails. Rooting from the sidelines while others took their chances in the field.

Brognola missed the firing line days. Sometimes he wished the clock and calendar could be reversed to put him back in the thick of the action.

And then, having wished it, he came to his senses.

Get it done, he thought, reaching out for the telephone once more.

Airborne over the Caribbean

THE LEARJET LONGHORN 60 handled like a dream. Grimaldi hardly had to work at the controls once he'd programmed their course and engaged the automatic pilot. He could sit back and enjoy the ride—except for the images playing in his mind.

He pictured Bolan, Johnny and Ross walking into an ambush in Nassau, unprepared for the guns and numbers they faced, shot to Hell in an instant, before he could help them. The scene played over and over again in his head, an endless video loop with slight but horrific variations in each screening.

Stop it!

They were safe for now, resting in the cabin behind him.

The Learjet cruised at an average speed of 523 miles per hour. The distance from Puerto Limón to Nassau, with a diversion to avoid Cuban airspace, was almost exactly 1,200 miles. Call it two hours and change between takeoff and touchdown, if all went according to plan.

Grimaldi scanned the vast blue sky in front of him, then checked his radar. Nothing. He hadn't expected bogies, of course. The enemy had no air force; they wouldn't have known where to find him in any case. Still, they were flying from one battle zone to another.

Their enemies were running, but only to a place where they felt safe. A place where they might stand their ground and fight next time, with lethal ferocity. Another battle was behind them, but the war went on.

Grimaldi knew exactly how the game was played, the same way he knew without checking that none of his passengers was catching up on much-needed sleep. They were most likely wide awake and thinking through the next phase of the killing game that lay ahead.

How badly had their enemies been damaged in the battles they'd already fought? Some hostile leaders had been taken out, but the opposition was still substantially intact, as far as Grimaldi could tell. Bolan's team hadn't seen the best of the enemy forces yet.

Or the worst.

A shadow fell across the control panel and Grimaldi half turned in his seat to find Bolan standing in the cockpit doorway. "Room for one more?" he asked.

Grimaldi nodded toward the empty copilot's seat. "As luck would have it."

Bolan settled in, checking a different angle on the bird's-eye view. "I make it ninety minutes, give or take," he said at last.

"Sounds right to me," Grimaldi agreed.

"I talked to Hal. He's checking out Sun's passengers and getting us a rundown on the current Nassau action. Also hardware outlets," Bolan said.

"The closer we get to home base," Grimaldi said, "the deeper they'll dig in."

"I'm counting on it. We've been chasing them too long, already."

"Right. There's that."

"No doubt about that," Bolan answered. "I hope you didn't feel sidelined last night."

"I'm not that sensitive, guy. Just give me a piece of the action when you can."

"Will do. In fact, it may be sooner than expected."

"Yeah?" Grimaldi didn't want to smile, but couldn't help himself.

"Could be," Bolan replied. "I won't know until we see what's happening in Nassau. If they make a stand, we'll need the big guns."

"This won't make it," said Grimaldi, fanning the air with one hand to indicate the unarmed Learjet.

"I'll see what we can do when the time comes," Bolan replied.

"Suits me."

"I guess I'd better catch some sack time." Bolan rose from his seat.

Alone again with the controls, Grimaldi watched the sky and ocean, calm and limitless from where he sat. On the surface, though, he knew there could be wind-whipped waves, rip tides, maybe a prowling school of sharks.

You never really knew by looking at the surface.

Soon they'd be immersed again and searching for hidden predators.

Grimaldi smiled, no hiding it this time.

He couldn't wait.

THERE WAS NO CUDDLING on the plane, with four window seats on each side and a narrow aisle down the middle, but Johnny supposed he and Keely Ross would've chosen separate seats in any case. They needed private time right now to put their thoughts in order and to prepare for the ordeal ahead with no distractions.

Johnny had no doubts that it would be an ordeal.

Their quarry had bolted from New Orleans, from Miami, and now from Panama City—but they couldn't run forever. Each time the enemy retreated, losing more men in the process, they moved closer to a final showdown that would determine the outcome of the game.

It was still a game, at some level, although the pieces in play were made of flesh and blood. When Johnny removed one from the board—or if he was himself removed—it meant death and destruction. There was no rewind, no instant replay, no last-minute saves. Players kept score in blood, and there was no provision for time-outs.

The hell of it was that he still wasn't sure of the stakes.

One thing was clear: high-ranking mobsters from around the world had formed some kind of coalition to support—and to control?—a revolution on Isla de Victoria. Maxwell Reed was their man, bought and paid for, even if he didn't recognize that fact himself.

The benefits of a mob-run country were obvious. They included tax breaks or exemptions, tight-lipped bankers, refuge from extradition treaties, and a potential gold rush from tourism à la Meyer Lansky's old spreads in Havana and Nassau. But that might only be the tip of the iceberg. With nation-state status, an underworld consortium could smuggle drugs and weapons, fugitives and slaves, a world of stolen property. It could field spies and hit teams, offer sanctuary to deposed tyrants, and generally operate outside the scope of international law.

What if they failed?

No sweat, Johnny decided. Hal Brognola was on the case, with Stony Man behind him—and, by extension, the whole U.S. government. Whatever happened in the next few hours or days, the scheduled transformation of Isla de Victoria into a criminal haven would not succeed.

Johnny could only hope that he would be around to share the victory.

He thought about Brent Schaefer, his friend from Army Ranger days who had come back into his life for a brief, violent moment in Mexico, nearly three weeks earlier. Schaefer's murder and his dying words had launched Johnny Gray on the trail that had brought him to his present point in time, winging eastward across the blue Caribbean at eighteen thousand feet without a cloud in the sky.

But the stormfront would be waiting for him when he landed in Nassau. The heavies didn't know he was coming yet—couldn't know Johnny's name or the identities of his companions—but they would be waiting nonetheless. They'd have no choice after suffering brutal setbacks in three successive venues, after losing so many men and so much prestige.

Saving face was a bitch, but it still counted for something, whether at the Pentagon or in the councils of the Yakuza, the

GET FREE BOOKS and a FREE GIFT WHEN YOU PLAY THE...

SLOT MACHINE GAME!

Just scratch off the silver box with a coin. Then check below to see the gifts you get!

YES!

I have scratched off the silver box. Please send me the 2 free Gold Eagle® books and gift for which I qualify. I understand I am under no obligation to purchase any books, as explained on the back of this card.

366 ADL D34F   **166 ADL D34E**

FIRST NAME   LAST NAME

ADDRESS

APT.#   CITY

STATE/PROV.   ZIP/POSTAL CODE

7	7	7	**Worth TWO FREE BOOKS plus a BONUS Mystery Gift!**
🍒	🍒	🍒	**Worth TWO FREE BOOKS!**
♣	♣	♣	**Worth ONE FREE BOOK!**
🔔	🔔	🍒	**TRY AGAIN!**

(MB-04-R)

(left margin, vertical) **DETACH AND MAIL CARD TODAY!**

The Gold Eagle Reader Service™ — Here's how it works:

Accepting your 2 free books and mystery gift places you under no obligation to buy anything. You may keep the books and gift and return the shipping statement marked "cancel." If you do not cancel, about a month later we'll send you 6 additional books and bill you just $29.94* — that's a saving of over 10% off the cover price of all 6 books! And there's no extra charge for shipping! You may cancel at any time, but if you choose to continue, every other month we'll send you 6 more books, which you may either purchase at the discount price or return to us and cancel your subscription.
*Terms and prices subject to change without notice. Sales tax applicable in N.Y. Canadian residents will be charged applicable provincial taxes and GST. Credit or debit balances in a customer's account(s) may be offset by any other outstanding balance owed by or to the customer.

Mafia, the Triads. Respect, however men defined it, was still a prerequisite of power.

"How are you?" someone asked him from his left. He turned to find that Keely Ross had shifted forward from her seat in the back to take the one across the aisle from Johnny.

"Fine," he said. "Woolgathering."

"I doubt it," she said, smiling. "You're planning how to handle it. I know you that well, anyway."

"Okay. I was just thinking that I'd like to see how this turns out." Johnny shrugged.

"You will," Ross said.

"Is that a guarantee?"

"Damn straight." She wasn't smiling now.

"I'll take it to the bank."

"Do that. We'll see the other side of this. I've set my mind on it."

"I hope that's all it takes."

Ross smiled again and sank back in her seat.

"Me, too," she said, turning to watch the ocean far below them through a pane of Plexiglas. And then again, for emphasis, "Me, too."

8

Nassau, Bahamas

Garrett Tripp was nervous as he waited for the elevator, checking out foot traffic in the lobby of the Royal Nassau Hotel. The "beautiful people" were all glitz and no substance in Tripp's opinion, but their futures looked brighter than his.

Much had happened since he'd last confronted his employers and argued successfully in favor of his own survival. None of those events had been Tripp's fault, but while he'd been powerless to prevent them, that didn't mean some mobster with a hard-on for revenge or personal advancement wouldn't take it out on him.

The summons had come not from Sun Zu-Wang, but from Pablo Aznar, speaking on behalf of Hector Santiago in Medellin. The Colombian *narcotraficantes* were well established throughout the Bahamas, and if their influence failed to match that of the Triads in Panama, it was simply a matter of degree.

Either one could squash him like an insect, on a whim.

It was Tripp's task—again—to make them see that he was worth more to their syndicate alive than feeding fish or rotting in a shallow grave.

If only he could pull it off a second time.

The Russians were his enemies. Tripp took that for granted. The rest had voted him a second chance, but some of them might reconsider their decision after the beating Sun's people had taken in Panama City.

Not my fault, Tripp reminded himself.

Unfortunately, being in the right didn't make him bulletproof. It wouldn't save his life.

For that, he needed guts and wits.

The elevator took him up to Aznar's penthouse on the thirteenth floor. Tripp wasn't superstitious, but he still couldn't help wondering if he had run out of luck.

The sliding door hissed open to reveal a pair of lanky shooters dressed in suits that must have cost a thousand dollars each. Both carried submachine guns slung across their shoulders, thereby wrinkling the expensive jackets. One of them produced a flat black wand and nodded for Tripp to assume the position.

Tripp raised his arms and waited while the Colombian scanned him for weapons. The shooters didn't frisk him, thereby missing both the fiberglass dagger sheathed inside the left sleeve of his sport coat and the razor-edged knuckle duster, molded from identical material, in his right hip pocket.

Tripp knew he might die today, but if it came to that, he meant to go down fighting. And he'd take as many of the bastards with him as he could.

Tripp's escort led him to a door without a number, thus confirming his suspicion that the penthouse was the sole accommodation on the hotel's thirteenth floor. He didn't know how space was allocated, how the sprawling suite of rooms was organized. There'd been no way for him to obtain advance intelligence.

But the cartel would either vote to kill him or allow him to proceed with his assigned duties. If it was death, the penthouse layout wouldn't matter.

All he'd need to find was Aznar's throat.

Inside the suite, Tripp followed his gun-toting guide past more guards through a parlor of sorts and into a formal meeting room. Facing him as he entered, from their seats at a broad conference table, were the same men who had given him a pass in Panama—plus one.

Maxwell Reed.

The gang's all here, thought Tripp.

He had considered smiling, but decided it was inappropriate. Instead he simply took the seat they'd left for him and listened for the door to close behind him when his escort left the room.

Without preamble, Aznar said, "You've heard about the trouble in Panama City."

It wasn't a question, but Tripp answered anyway. "Yes."

"Your people were still in the air when it happened."

"Yes, sir. As I'd told you they would be, until midnight."

"You understand," Semyon Borodin interrupted his host, "how bad this looks for you?"

"I must be missing something," Tripp replied, stone-faced. "I made it clear how long my people needed to fly in and reinforce the agreed upon sites. The raid came two hours before that, and Mr. Sun's private residence wasn't on the list of targets they were supposed to protect." Turning to Sun, he added, "That was your decision, sir, not mine. You left home base security to Mr. Chiang."

"Chiang's dead," Sun told him.

"So I understand. I'm sorry that the raid went down the way it did. But once again, it isn't my responsibility."

"Suppose we make it yours?" the Russian prodded him.

"Then you'd be making a mistake." No *sir* this time.

"Is that a threat?" Borodin wore a ravenous smile.

"It's a statement of fact. You didn't get what you have today by misjudging people or killing off those who can help you."

"You have no idea who I've killed."

"Okay. I thought you were a man of wisdom. Maybe I was wrong."

Borodin blinked at him, trying to decide if he had been insulted. Tripp left him to it and addressed the others, trusting them to swing the vote against his adversary as they had before. If he could hold them on his side.

"You face a risk today," he said, "much worse than anything you've seen since this campaign began. Somebody has your number and they're pressing hard to bring you down. We don't know who they are, but there's a way of finding out."

"Which is?" Aznar was calm, almost aloof. Except for Borodin, still brooding, the remainder of the jury seemed to take their cue from him.

"Which is," Tripp said, "to capture one of them and squeeze him until he sings. If we identify the opposition, I can beat them."

"Capture one of them." Tanaka made no effort to conceal his skepticism. "After all this time, how would you manage that?"

"All right," Tripp said. "Here's what I have in mind."

THE LAYOUT LOOKED familiar. Déjà vu. It was a new hotel room in a different city with brand-new weapons laid out on a bed he'd never seen before, but Jack Grimaldi couldn't escape the sense that he'd been here before.

They'd gone shopping for hardware soon after checking into one of Nassau's midrange resort hotels.

Hal Brognola was still piecing together dossiers on Maxwell Reed's criminal sponsors, but he'd needed less time to conjure up the name and address of a Bahamian arms merchant.

The dealer was Jamaican, once removed. He didn't have the inventory of the vendor who'd supplied them in Panama City, but his stock-on-hand was adequate for their needs. They had picked up two SA-80 assault rifles, two M-P5 A3 submachine guns, and four SIG-Sauer P-226 semiautomatic pistols. Their choice of frag grenades were the latest British L109A1s. Spare magazines and ammunition completed the purchase, taking a fair bite out of Bolan's war chest.

But money was the last thing on Grimaldi's mind.

Bolan had gone out to find a pay phone for his callback to Brognola. Grimaldi, Ross and Johnny had been left to strip the weapons and inspect them, making sure they were ready to rock on demand.

"I have a bad feeling on this one," Johnny remarked as he loaded magazines for the SA-80s.

Frowning, Grimaldi glanced up from his reassembly of an SMG. "You mean, as opposed to all the good feelings we've had lately?"

"Different," Johnny said. "It's like… Forget it."

"No. I trust your gut."

"It's nothing I can put a finger on," Johnny replied. "Hell, we haven't done anything yet. It just feels like trouble."

"We came for trouble," Grimaldi reminded him.

"I know." Johnny nodded, still loading, and repeated, "I know."

"The trick is making sure their trouble's worse than ours."

"And getting out alive," Ross added, sitting with a newly reassembled auto pistol in her nimble hands. "Let's not forget that."

"No, ma'am," Grimaldi answered her, shaking his head. "I'm not forgetting that." But in his heart, he knew that sometimes getting out alive just wasn't in the cards.

Solemn but resigned, he went back to work on the sleek SMG.

"HE'S SLICK, THAT AMERICAN. Always saying just what you want to hear."

Semyon Borodin drew deeply on his cheroot, watching Aznar's face as the Colombian sipped a glass of Bahamian beer. He had lingered in Aznar's penthouse when the others dispersed to their separate suites, craving another chance for private conversation with the man from Medellin.

"Maybe he says the right thing because he is right," Aznar replied. His smile hung somewhere between thoughtful and mocking.

"What?" Borodin feigned surprise. "You believed him?"

"I voted to give him a chance. So did you."

Borodin fanned the air with his hand, trailing smoke. "That's all politics," he said. "Nobody wants to be the odd man out and start a feeding frenzy."

"Worried, are you?"

"For myself?" The Russian frowned and shook his head. "Not me. I'm a survivor. Just like you, Pablo."

Did he imagine it or had Aznar grimaced at the use of his first name? Too familiar? The Colombian took another sip of beer and said, "No one survives forever."

"Are you volunteering for the chop?"

"What do you think?"

"I've already said it. You're a born survivor, just like me. You'll let the others go to Hell before you sacrifice yourself."

"That doesn't sound like an alliance," Aznar said.

"It's an alliance of convenience," said Borodin. "When was it ever more than that? It's not as if we're family, after all."

"But partners," the Colombian replied.

"Of course. Equal in theory."

"And in fact?"

Borodin shrugged. "We're all strong men with guns behind us. That's a given. We'd be dead by now, otherwise, yes?"

Aznar did not reply.

"The difference," Borodin continued, "lies in the nature of our respective strengths—and weaknesses."

"Whose weaknesses are you referring to?" Aznar inquired.

Another shrug, so casual. Borodin drew on his smoke, savored it, then stubbed the cheroot out in a crystal ashtray the size of a hubcap.

"Whose?" he echoed. "No one in particular. Of course, these Asians—" he waved again, a dismissive gesture "—who knows what they're thinking."

"What would you do with them?" Aznar was sly, watching.

"For now? Nothing. They're useful in their way. Good sources, good contacts. Good cannon fodder."

"Ah."

"You haven't thought the same thing, even once?"

"It may have crossed my mind," Aznar allowed.

"I knew it." Borodin smiled. "But for the moment, naturally, appearances must be preserved."

Aznar finished his beer and set the empty glass aside. "Of course," he said. No smile.

For a moment Borodin feared that he'd said too much. If he had misjudged the Colombian, if Aznar was closer to Sun and Tanaka than Borodin supposed, then Borodin might have signed his own death warrant with a smile.

All life was a risk, with the measure of rewards based on the danger faced in gaining them. Borodin had learned that lesson as a child, it stayed with him still.

"And Tripp?" Aznar pressed.

"Let him do his job, if he can," the Russian answered. "But if he fails again…" Borodin left the sentence hanging but raised a hand and drew his index finger sharply across his own gullet.

"It's no more than we voted this morning," Aznar observed.

"You see? I'm keeping faith."

For now, Semyon Borodin thought.

BOLAN STOOD IN THE TROPICAL heat, barely shaded by the sidewalk telephone booth. He waited, watching traffic while he listened to another phone ringing in Washington, eight hundred miles away.

Brognola picked up on the third ring. "Speak to me."

"That's my line," Bolan answered.

"Right. Okay. Are we secure."

"I hope so."

Bolan heard a faint riffle of paper as Brognola said, "All right, then. Let's run through those names. You want them alphabetically?"

"Whatever."

"A is for Aznar," Brognola said. "First name Pablo. The DEA lists him as second-in-command to a bull stud named Hector Santiago, out of Medellin. They move a lot of marching powder north by different routes, with Nassau being one of the stopovers."

"No surprise."

"I didn't think so. Santiago's down with DEA and the Bureau as the new Pablo Escobar. Billions to burn, and Bogota can't seem to find him when it's extradition time. That's probably because his 12,000-acre estate and his 60-room house are so easy to miss."

"You think?"

"I gave up thinking for Lent. Anyway, Santiago and Aznar don't *own* the Bahamian government yet, but it sounds like they're leasing with an option to buy. You're basically on their turf now."

"Duly noted," said Bolan.

"Next up, B for Borodin, Semyon. He fought his way up from the streets in Leningrad—make that St. Petersburg—and made his first million rubles smuggling Turkish heroin into the Soviet worker's paradise. Did some time in his twenties, but bought his way out of the Gulag before they could lose him. Since 91 Borodin's been among the top players. He backed Yeltsin, then cut his losses when the time was right. He's into everything but temperance and moderation."

"That leaves Tanaka," Bolan said.

"It does, indeed. He's Yakuza, just like we thought. His family rules the roost in Kobe, but they're looking to expand. He's learned to live and let live with the Triads when it matters, most particularly Sun Zu-Wang's White Lotus faction. Deals in Hong Kong, Singapore, Sri Lanka—and a little piece of Vegas, for variety."

"Vegas?" Bolan had heard of Yakuza investments in Nevada gambling some years ago, but nothing recently.

"One of his cousins has points in a place on the Strip. The Midas Touch, that is. More ways than one, I guess."

"No more Sicilians?" Bolan asked his old friend.

"Not so fast. You know Dante Ambrosio?"

"The old man from Calabria?"

"The very same," Brognola said. "Turns out he's tight with Borodin and Aznar, both. I ran a check on overseas phone traffic through the NSA and came up with calls between Ambrosio and Sun Zu-Wang in Panama City. Most recently, yesterday afternoon."

"A full house then."

"In spades."

"Does Ambrosio have people in Nassau?"

"I'm checking that now," Brognola replied. "So far, he looks more like some kind of long-distance investor, standing by to claim his slice of the pie when it's out of the oven."

"They may have too many chefs," Bolan said.

"Wish I could help you stir the pot." Brognola sounded wistful.

"Maybe next time. Right now, I need local addresses if you've got them."

Brognola shuffled some papers, then recited the names of four top-range hotels, matching each to a name or names from the hit list.

"That should do it," Bolan said when he finished.

"Right. The hardware deal went down okay, I guess?"

"No problems."

"Good. I'll let you go then. Give 'em Hell."

"It's on the menu."

Bolan broke the link and walked back to his rental car. It was already hot as Hell, or getting there. But it would be a good deal hotter, very soon.

A dose of cleansing fire was on its way.

MAXWELL REED SAT WAITING to receive a message from the Lord, but God was not responding at the moment. It galled Reed when the Almighty put him on hold—but what could he do except wait?

"Your excellency?"

The voice wasn't God's, but it cut through the haze. Reed blinked several times, rapidly, and turned to find his aide de camp, Merrill Harris, watching him closely.

"What is it, Merrill?"

Harris frowned as if perplexed by the question, but he quickly recovered. "Your meeting with the sponsors, sir. I've just come to remind you that it's almost time."

"Meeting? Of course," he said. "When will they be here?"

Harris's frown seemed to deepen. "We must go to them, sir," he replied.

Reed took the news calmly. "What is the time, Merrill?" he asked.

Harris checked his wristwatch. "It's half past eleven, sir."

"We should be going, then."

"Yes, sir. The car's downstairs."

It was a dreamy sort of ride, at first, but cruel reality sank in on Reed before the pale gray limousine had reached its destination. He remembered why he was in Nassau, why he'd tried so desperately to glean some message from the Lord before he had to face his so-called "friends," the men who had convinced themselves that they controlled Reed's life, his very destiny.

He had a rude surprise in store for some of them.

But he needed their continuing support to survive and realize his goal. When he was safely installed in the president's mansion on Isla de Victoria, then and only then would Reed reveal his true face, his true power, to the men who thought he was their pawn.

But none of that would happen if his enemies—still faceless, nameless, despite all they'd done—managed to overtake him and destroy his dream. In that case it would all have been a waste of time.

But how could God be wrong?

That quandary kept Reed occupied until they reached their destination. His security personnel left the vehicle first, scanning the sidewalk with professional eyes. One man went ahead to check the hotel lobby for potential danger, returning to say it was clear. Reed took his time emerging from the limousine, then made his way inside, surrounded by bodyguards. He guessed that none who watched him pass knew who he was, and that was fine. Reed wasn't interested in fame.

It was power that mattered.

More guards—not his—were waiting when Reed's party reached its destination on the seventh floor. As the door closed behind them, the muscle left Reed with a guide who led him to a kind of makeshift conference room where Kenji Tanaka and Sun Zu-Wang awaited him.

"Where are the others?" Reed inquired.

"They won't be joining us," Tanaka said. "Please, sit."

Reed sat, as if he was their faithful dog. Smiling.

Waiting.

"We hope that everything is satisfactory at your hotel," Sun said by way of preamble.

"It is."

"If there is anything you need…?"

"Nothing, so far." Reed knew they could've asked these questions on the telephone. There must be something else, something more urgent on their minds.

"You are aware," Tanaka said, "that we've instructed Tripp to augment your personal security?"

"I have his guards waiting outside," Reed said.

"Indeed. But if there is another *incident*—" Sun spoke the word as if it left a foul taste in his mouth "—we shall be forced to dispense with his services."

"Ah."

Tanaka's turn. "We trust you have no objection?"

"None," Reed replied. "Success is paramount. If Tripp can't do his job, he has no value."

"There's a risk," Sun said, "that losing him may cause some delay in liberating your homeland."

"There will be no delay," Reed told them confidently.

"But—"

"The Lord will not allow it," he informed them.

For the first time since Reed had entered the room, Sun and Tanaka exchanged glances. Their faces were dead-pan, waxen. When they smiled simultaneously, their expressions seemed rehearsed, artificial.

"I'm glad to see you so confident," Tanaka said.

"We were afraid that you might be discouraged," Sun added.

Reed laughed at that. He simply couldn't help himself. "Discouraged? Not a bit! Setbacks are only natural, but I will have my victory," he said. "It has been preordained."

"In that case, there's no reason for concern," Tanaka said. "Why don't we have some sake and relax?"

They think I'm mad, Reed thought. So much the better.

If they thought he was a madman or a simpleton, it would be that much easier to take them by surprise when Reed no longer needed them.

That day was coming. It would soon be here.

"I'd like a cup of sake," he told Tanaka, smiling. "Thank you very much."

PABLO AZNAR WAS ON HOLD for nearly two minutes before Hector Santiago came on the line. Aznar assumed that Santiago had been enjoying his usual matinee with Rosita, his mistress of the moment. It was that time of day, and Hector sounded slightly out of breath when first he spoke.

"Pablo, *¿qué tal?*"

"We have a problem, Hector."

"Tripp, again?" There was a weary note to Santiago's voice.

"Besides that."

"Ah. The Russian?"

"*Sí.* He's still agitating for Tripp's job, in charge of security."

"We could get rid of him, Pablo."

Aznar had already considered that option. "A war in the ranks wouldn't help us right now," he replied.

"The only reason for a war," said Santiago, "is if someone knows we did it, *sí.*"

Aznar shrugged, then remembered that he had to speak to communicate. "What are you saying?" he asked.

"Suppose we let these bastards who are causing all the trouble deal with Borodin? There'd be no reason for a war, in that case."

He was about to say, "We don't know who they are," but then he understood what Santiago meant. "It just might work."

"Who knows, until we try?"

"Shall I proceed, then?"

"Use your own discretion," Santiago said. "You have my every confidence."

"In that case—"

"Just be careful. Nothing traceable to us, no matter what you do."

"Of course."

"Anything else that I should know about?"

"Nothing at the moment."

"Good. Then I'll get back to the gymnasium."

Rosita, Aznar thought again.

Aznar smiled as he imagined taking care of Borodin once and for all. It would require a measure of finesse, but he couldn't put it off for very long. If something happened in the meantime and their unknown adversaries were identified and eliminated, it would ruin everything.

Aznar pressed a button on his office intercom and spoke a name. Seconds later, a young man stood in front of him.

Aznar spelled it out for the gunman. He didn't try to work out any of the details, believing that a good commander should trust his soldiers to show some initiative. Twice he stressed the importance of secrecy, of covering tracks. When he was done, the young man smiled and asked him simply, "When?"

"Tonight, if possible. No later than tomorrow night, in any case."

"It's done," the soldier said, and left Aznar alone.

Pablo Aznar felt better already.

"WHY THE RUSSIAN?" asked Johnny when Bolan had laid out his plan for the evening's offensive.

"A little change of pace," Bolan answered. "I'd like to throw Aznar off guard, maybe cause a few stress cracks in the alliance. Then again, maybe we'll find somebody we can squeeze for information."

"What about Reed?" Ross inquired.

"We'll get him. But I'm more concerned about the men behind the scenes and what they're getting out of this. Reed's the beard. I plan on cutting off the head."

"When do we case the hotel?" Johnny asked.

"Dry run as soon as we get finished here," Bolan replied.

"We'll check out the security as far as possible, and run the main event later tonight."

"There'll be a problem with civilians," Ross reminded him.

"Less on the graveyard shift than any other time," Bolan observed. "I'd rather have them off alone, somewhere, but they haven't given us that choice. We'll take precautions. Try to keep it surgical."

He'd already considered trying to lure the enemy out into the open, away from the downtown hotels, but thus far Bolan had no bargaining chips. That might change if he laid hands on Semyon Borodin—or, at least he might gain some new battlefield intelligence to help them make the next strike cleaner, more precise.

There was no doubt there would be a next strike and perhaps another after that. Borodin was part of the cabal, but nothing suggested he ran the show or held any controlling share of the action. Removing him most likely wouldn't cripple Bolan's remaining enemy, but it might slow them down. And if Borodin could be persuaded to tell what he knew about the ongoing conspiracy, who knew what sort of an advantage it might give Bolan's team.

If he refused to talk…well, he would still be neutralized.

"Is this dry run a dress rehearsal?" Ross asked Bolan. Meaning, would they go in fully armed or simply scout the place for future reference?

"A soft probe ought to do it," Bolan said. "No one who's seen us is around to talk about it, so I'm not expecting anyone to point a finger."

"In that case," she told him, "I'm ready to go."

"Same here," Johnny said.

Grimaldi set his Uzi on the bed, using a paper towel to wipe his hands, and added, "Ditto."

Bolan examined his companions, one face at a time. They were weary but willing, grim-faced and going for broke. He knew what his brother and Grimaldi were made of, and Bolan had seen enough of Keely Ross in action to figure that she wouldn't let him down. As for the aftermath—and anything that might go wrong with the hotel raid—they would simply have to live with it.

Bolan didn't know exactly what was going on between Ross and his brother, and he didn't plan to ask. If they could find a private moment and make it their own in the midst of so much death, more power to them. He'd been there himself, once upon a time, but it had been so long that Bolan had almost forgotten the feeling.

Tonight, he had another kind of feeling.

Blood and fire, the killing kind.

It was the only way he knew to play this game and, as long as it worked, he had no great incentive to change.

Bolan hoped he'd come out on the other side with everyone who'd joined him at the starting line. If not...

Well, there was always Hell enough to go around.

9

Guillermo Calderon enjoyed the last moment of calm before a firestorm—but he preferred the storm itself. He loved the noise and the chaotic action. The smell of burned gunpowder even reminded him of celebrations in his native Colombian village, like fireworks popping in the street.

Killing was better, though, because he controlled the fireworks.

Eight men surrounded Calderon in the hotel parking lot. One of the hotel's security floodlights was dark now, allowing them a measure of privacy as Calderon went over the plan one last time. Heads bobbed around the silent circle as he finished running down the details. None of them was big on conversation, but their eyes told him everything Calderon needed to know.

They were ready.

Despite the heat, each member of the team—including Calderon—wore long black dusters to conceal the hardware they carried underneath. They had a mix of automatic weapons, no particular criteria for selection beyond a shooter's preference. Calderon's choice for the evening was a mini-Uzi with a foot-long sound suppressor and two 32-round magazines clipped into an L-shape for easy reloading on the run. More magazines weighted his coat pockets, while his sidearm—an Argentine Ballester-Molina .45 caliber automatic, sat heavy in a holster beneath his right arm.

"Let's go, then," he ordered, and moved from the shadows across the hotel parking lot. They slipped through the service entrance without meeting any opposition, heading for the big freight elevator.

Calderon understood that the Russian had at least a dozen bodyguards, some his own men, others supplied by the gringo Tripp, who also served Calderon's master. Calderon didn't know why Aznar wanted him to kill the Russians and the gringo's men, nor did he care. It was enough to carry out the order and to be rewarded for a job well done.

It was approaching midnight when they reached the elevator, late for room service and housekeeping to have their people moving between floors. No one passed by while they waited for the elevator car to ascend from its resting place in the basement. There was no one on board when they entered the plain, sterile car and Calderon pushed the button for Borodin's floor.

Calderon drew the Uzi from under his coat, leaving it clipped to its chamois shoulder harness as he racked the slide to put a live round in the chamber. For a moment the elevator car was filled with sharp, metallic sounds of weapons being cocked, then deathly silence fell again. They passed the fifth, sixth, seventh floors without a spoken word.

The elevator stopped on eight, as Calderon had planned. From that point to the tenth floor, they would use the stairs. There was less risk of being ambushed that way, and a better chance of taking Borodin's watchdogs by surprise.

"Come on!" Calderon snapped as he left the elevator car and crossed the spacious corridor to reach the stairs. "Stay with me now. We're on the clock."

No answer from his soldiers. They would do as they were told or die in the attempt.

Climbing the stairs with gun in hand, he simply had to smile.

BOLAN WAS ALMOST LATE, because he didn't know there was a party going on. He'd planned the strike for half-past midnight, which meant moving in ahead of time, but there were shooters on the scene before his team arrived. He didn't know it, even then, until he found the first stiff on the service stairs.

The guy was freshly dead, cut down by several gunshots to the head and chest. He sprawled across four steps, head down, blood dribbling from the risers like some kind of scarlet waterfall.

"This can't be good," Grimaldi said, behind him.

Speaking through his microphone, to Ross and Johnny in the elevator, Bolan said, "Heads up. Somebody got here first. We have one KIA."

"Copy," his brother's voice came back.

Bolan stepped around the body, careful with his footing on the bloody stairs. He thought they must've nearly met the other shooters on the stairs—and then he heard gunfire, one floor above.

"Trouble!" he said into the slender stalk protruding from his headpiece, almost kissing close. "We have gunfire on ten. Repeat, gunfire on ten."

"Are we aborting?" Johnny asked.

"Not yet. I want to check it out."

"Affirmative. We're almost there."

The door in front of him had a large number 10 painted on it, with instructions below to Keep This Door Closed At All Times. That fire precaution was unrelated to the kind of fire Bolan heard echoing from the hallway just beyond the door.

He hesitated for a heartbeat, and Grimaldi asked him, "Are we going for it?"

Bolan held his SA-80 tight against his ribs and said, "It's why we're here."

Grimaldi smiled and raised the muzzle of his MP-5. "All right," he said. "I've got your back."

Bolan opened the door with his left hand, holding the assault rifle steady with his right. The smell of cordite, already present in the stairwell slaughterhouse, grew stronger as he stepped across the threshold and onto the tenth floor proper. Grimaldi was close behind him, easing the door shut without a perceptible sound.

Not that anyone would've heard it, regardless. There was too much gunplay just beyond the corner that blocked Bolan's view. The entry to the fire stairs had been tucked into an alcove near the elevators, with an ice dispenser and multiple vending machines.

Bolan edged toward the corner and peered around it, glimpsing figures in motion before another burst of automatic fire raked the hallway.

"How many?" asked Grimaldi.

"One down, that I'm sure of. Hard to say how many on the move. At least a dozen, maybe more."

"Somebody's hitting Borodin?"

"Somebody *else*," Bolan corrected him.

"You wanna leave them to it?" Grimaldi inquired, flashing that smile again.

"It's still our game."

"We're late," Grimaldi said. "Could be a forfeit."

"Not this time."

"Okay, I'm with you."

Bolan spoke into the microphone again. "How close are you?" he asked.

"We're standing by," Johnny replied.

"You hear it?" Bolan asked his brother.

"Loud and clear."

"We've got a war in progress, unknown players on the strike team."

"Want to scrub it?" Johnny asked him.

"No. I'm going in. Say sixty seconds."

"Got it. See you there, bro'."

"Just one thing before we do it," said Grimaldi. "Who's the enemy out there?"

"They all are," Bolan said.

He checked the time, watching the numbers fall. At sixty seconds Bolan stepped around the corner, firing from the hip.

"WHO ARE THESE SONS of bitches?" Semyon Borodin demanded.

Nikolai Yurochka glared at him and answered, "How in Hell should I know?"

"You're *supposed* to know these things!"

"I didn't give the fuckers invitations, did I?"

Borodin knew he was being unreasonable, but his anger and fear overwhelmed simple logic. He was crouched behind the sofa with Yurochka, gripping his FN Five-seveN pistol so tightly that his knuckles were blanched deathly white. There'd been no targets yet, but the sounds of battle seemed to be drawing closer by the moment.

"I don't believe they found us here," Yurochka said. "It's too damned fast."

"You don't believe who found us, Nikolai?"

"The shits from Panama. It's only been a day since they were after Sun. How could they find us?"

"Who else would it be?" Before he even asked the question, though, Borodin had begun to list potential enemies.

And most of them were masquerading as his friends.

"We can't stay here," Yurochka said. "We're fish in a barrel unless we get out."

"You mean out there?"

Yurochka's smile had more in common with a grimace.

"Unless you want to try the window," he replied. "Ten stories down, I hope you packed your parachute."

"Goddamn it!"

"Are you with me, Semyon?"

"What choice do I have?"

This time, his old friend's smile had life to it. "You always have a choice," he said. "Go out with me, or sit and wait for someone to come knocking."

"All right," said Borodin. "Let's go."

He wasn't sure how many of his men were still alive, but they would have to do their best with what they had. Yurochka shouted orders in Russian to the nearest survivors, rallying them to their master. Borodin was the last to rise from hiding, waiting for the others to form a phalanx around him, shielding him with their bodies.

"Ready?" Yurochka asked.

"As ready as I'll ever be."

"All right. We'll pick up more along the way. Move out!"

At his command, the wedge formation started forward, moving with grim determination to the door and toward the battleground that lay beyond. Another moment would decide whether they lived or died.

Of one thing, Borodin was certain.

He would not go down without a fight.

JOHNNY LEFT THE ELEVATOR one step ahead of Keely Ross and dropped into a fighting crouch. The hotel elevators, like the service stairs, were set back from the hallway lined with guest rooms, positioned so that the chiming bells and hissing doors would cause only a minimal disturbance for the paying customers.

It was convenient for the guests, Johnny supposed, but he wished the architects had given some thought to security when they'd been hunched over their drawing boards. A convex mirror on the wall directly opposite would've been help-ful, for example, in providing a view of the hallway beyond.

As it was, though, Johnny had his first glimpse of the enemy as soon as he stepped from the elevator car. The man was kneeling at one corner of the elevator alcove, sneaking looks around the edge while he held an Uzi ready, finger on the trig-ger. At the sound of the elevator doors behind him, he lurched backward, swiveling to face the unexpected challenge.

Johnny read the shock on the stranger's face, but he didn't hesitate. He milked his SA-80 for a 3-round burst that stitched across the shooter's chest and punched him back into the open hallway. A longer burst of auto fire instantly took over, spinning the corpse and making it dance for a moment, before it collapsed.

"Jesus!"

He turned to find Ross at his elbow, staring at the body on the carpet. "There's more where he came from," Johnny remarked.

"I got that feeling," she replied.

"You ready?"

"Now or never."

Johnny moved to the spot the dead man had occupied sec-onds earlier and took his place. A hasty glance around the cor-ner was enough to show him a battleground littered with bodies, gunmen ducking in and out of sparse cover while ex-changing bursts of automatic fire. The walls were pocked with bullet holes, and somewhere, behind one of the num-bered doors, a woman was screaming nonstop.

"Who is it?" Ross asked him.

"Hell if I know. We've got ten or fifteen shooters going at it, and I don't see any friendly faces."

"Matt and Jack?"

"The service stairs are at the far end of the hall," he told her. "On the other side of all those guns."

She swallowed hard and said, "Okay. What are we wait-ing for?"

"Nothing," he answered.

Leaning back into the hallway, Johnny raised the SA-80 to his shoulder and began to fire at any target he could see.

BOLAN DUCKED A BURST of automatic fire, felt plaster raining down into his hair, and killed the shooter who had nearly taken off his head. The target went down thrashing, firing as he fell, his bullets ripping zigzag patterns in the ceiling tiles.

The firefight had become mobile, with Bolan in the midst of it. He had been separated from Grimaldi on the first rush; a gunner in a long black coat had cut loose on Grimaldi and driven him back to cover. Bolan had kept moving, dropped the shooter where he stood, and ducked into a recessed doorway half a dozen paces further on. It wasn't much, in terms of cover, but it was the best available.

Bolan had no idea who the raiders might be, or whether they'd already reached Borodin. For all he knew, the Russian could be dead, the rest of it a clumsy fighting withdrawal. In that case, he was wasting time and risking the lives of his teammates for nothing.

But before he pulled out, Bolan had to be sure.

That meant blitzing through the slaughter pen in front of him to locate Semyon Borodin, dead or alive.

Job One would be for him to clear a path.

Bolan palmed one of the L109A1 grenades, released its safety pin, and stepped from cover long enough to make the pitch. He threw it side-hand, toward the middle of the firefight. It was a considered move, well planned and executed.

There was nothing in his prior experience that could prepare him for what happened next.

The guy was fast, no doubt about it. One of the invaders, seemingly, he wore a jet-black duster that hung almost to his ankles. He was fighting with his back toward Bolan, then began to turn, perhaps reaching for a replacement magazine inside his coat. Half turned that way, he must have seen the Executioner emerge from hiding in the doorway as he'd lobbed the frag grenade.

It was the time to cut and run, to save himself, but this one did the very opposite. Without even a word of warning to his comrades, he ran *toward* the airborne hand grenade, dropping his gun to dangle from some kind of shoulder sling as he prepared to make the catch with outstretched hands. He could have been a center fielder for the Yankees, the way he snatched the lethal orb midair, spun around once to give himself momentum, and returned the pitch to Bolan with a snarl of triumph on his face.

It all happened so fast, Bolan hadn't had time to cut the guy down before he snagged the grenade and returned it. Then, with the bomb on its way back home, there was no point in shooting him. Bolan had to focus on survival, backpedaling desperately, huddling in the sparse shelter of his recessed doorway, hoping that most of the blast would go high and wide of the swift pitcher's mark.

Bolan almost made it.

The blast was like a draft from Hell, together with a drop kick from an angry giant. The concussion slammed Bolan head-on into wood and plaster, possibly a door frame, maybe just a wall. Gagging on smoke and dust, he toppled slowly backward, groping for his rifle as the world turned upside down and then winked out.

KEELY ROSS WINCED and recoiled as the grenade blast rocked the hotel corridor, clouds of smoke and dust swirling in its wake. She hesitated, reluctant to fire through that haze without marking clear targets, but Johnny unleashed a burst before the echoes of the blast had ceased reverberating from the walls around them.

"Good chance to clean them out," he said, firing another burst along the corridor.

Ross moved to his side, tracking the figures moving in the hallway as they lurched and loomed in front of her gunsights. Something was on fire, she smelled it now, distinct and separate from the stench of cordite and explosives. In another second, as if validating her suspicion, fire alarms began to clamor in the smoky corridor while sprinklers opened up above their heads and drenched the scene.

"Goddamn monsoon," said Johnny. He rose and moved in closer to the action, firing as he went.

Ross followed, watching for any shooters sprawled around the hallway who might suddenly decide to rise and join the fight anew. She didn't trust the faceless dead and didn't plan to let one of them shoot her in the back if she could possibly avoid it.

Sudden crackling in her ear distracted Ross. Grimaldi was saying something, but the rattling sounds of gunfire in her right ear and a hiss of static from the earpiece kept her from deciphering his words.

"Repeat, please!" she instructed him. "You're breaking up."

"I said—"

One of the bodies in her path chose that moment to lurch upright to aim a weapon at the back of Johnny's head. Ross wasted no time on a shouted warning. It was quicker just to hit the shooter with a stream of bullets from her MP-5 and put him down again, this time for good.

As she stood over him—a real corpse now, no doubt about it—Ross saw Johnny turn back to her, a dazed expression on his face. At first she thought that he'd been hit. Then Johnny moved in close enough to speak.

"Did you hear that?" he asked.

She shook her head and pointed to the shooter she'd just killed. "What did Jack say?"

"We have to hurry. Mack's been hurt. They've got him."

"Mack?" She was confused. "Who's *Mack?*"

Johnny blinked twice, recovering a bit from the initial shock. "It's Matt. He's hurt, somehow. The opposition has him."

"Jesus! Where?"

He turned and pointed through the pall of drifting smoke. "Somewhere down there."

"We can't just rush ahead and—"

"Stay here if you want to," Johnny cut her off. "I have to help him now, while there's still time."

And saying that, he ran headlong into the battle, charging like a madman to his doom.

THE HOTEL WAS BURNING—or was that simply battle smoke that hung so thickly in the corridor? Semyon Borodin wasn't sure, and he didn't really care as long as he got out of the damned place in one piece. All around him, guns were still firing, bullets slapping into ceilings, walls and flesh. Each passing second made escape seem less likely, sudden death more probable.

Borodin held a handkerchief in his left hand, pressed against his mouth and nose as a kind of crude gas mask, while he clutched his pistol in his right. He hadn't fired the weapon but his finger was tight on the trigger, aching with the desire to share some of the death that surrounded him.

Better them than me, the Russian thought, knowing all too well that it could still be him at any moment.

As if to prove the point, one of his soldiers stumbled, slumped against the wall and slithered to the floor. He left a bright red stain on the wallpaper, where blood had fountained from an exit wound. Borodin ducked lower, using his body-guards as human shields, and glanced around to see if Yurochka was still keeping pace.

He was a few steps behind Borodin's little group, crouching beside a body that lay huddled in one of the corridor's many recessed doorways.

Borodin shouted at him, trying to be heard above the gunfire. "Nicolai! What are you doing?"

Peering through the battle haze, Yurochka answered, "You should see this one."

"I've seen enough already, dammit!"

"Not like this one."

Nicolai was careful not to use Borodin's name, a sensible precaution in the circumstances, but he held his ground beside the corpse.

Borodin considered leaving his lieutenant to the jackals, but he trusted Yurochka's instincts. If this was something that would help him stay alive—

Snarling curses, Borodin herded his bodyguards back toward the doorway where Yurochka knelt. They returned fire sporadically, mostly aiming at shadows now, as the firefight degenerated into random sniping. The fire alarm clamored on, combining with the stench of smoke to threaten Borodin with a migraine headache.

He reached the body, knelt beside it— and saw what Yurochka meant. This one wasn't dressed like the others who'd stormed his hotel suite. He lacked their oily hair and swarthy features. Borodin bent closer, prepared to frisk the body—and recoiled when it moved beneath his hand.

"He's still alive!"

Yurochka nodded. "We could take him with us. Find somewhere to question him."

It was a snap decision, under circumstances where any delay could be fatal. "Do it!" Borodin ordered. Then, to his soldiers, "Hurry up! He's coming with us. And make damned sure he's unarmed."

They stripped the large, unconscious man of weapons. Seconds later, two of Borodin's men hoisted the stranger by his armpits and made for the nearest exit, dragging him between them so that his heels scraped the carpet. Borodin followed close behind them, Yurochka at his side.

"You've done well, Nicolai," he said.

Yurochka shrugged, turning to watch the corridor behind them, ever on alert. "Maybe it's not all wasted, anyway."

"Don't worry." Borodin was smiling. It felt good, and took him by surprise. "Before I'm finished with our friend, he'll tell us everything we need to know and beg us for the opportunity to sell his closest friends."

They reached the fire stairs, waited while the soldiers checked and found the exit clear, then passed through in a rush and started on the long trek down.

GUILLERMO CALDERON KNEW when he was beaten, but knowing it and disengaging from a hopeless fight were very different things.

Somehow, in the heat of the action, Calderon and two of his men had managed to penetrate Borodin's suite—but the Russian had already gone and they were now trapped inside his room.

No, that was overstating it. They were pinned down for the moment, but it didn't mean their situation was hopeless. Despite everything, Calderon believed they could fight their way back to the stairs or the freight elevator.

Scratch that.

The elevators would've shut down as soon as the fire alarm sounded. It was an automatic precaution in modern hotels, to prevent guests from being trapped and baked in the cars in the event of a blaze.

The stairs, then. Calderon preferred them, in any case. If only he could reach them alive, avoid enemies on his way to the street, and escape before the neighborhood was crawling with Bahamian police.

"We're getting out of here," he told his men.

The older of them, Rodriguez, scowled at Calderon and said, "How are we doing it?"

"I only see one door," said Calderon.

"That's your plan?"

"Or we could sit and wait for the police to smoke us out. They hang killers here, but maybe you'll get lucky and they'll only sentence you to life in prison."

Rodriguez shook his head. Whether to clear it or in disagreement, Calderon could not have said. A moment later the gunman replied, "All right. Who goes first?"

"I'll go," said Roberto Garcia, the younger of Calderon's shooters. "It's better than nothing."

"So, do it," Calderon commanded.

Garcia flashed a brilliant smile and rushed the doorway, lunging through it and into the hallway beyond. More shooting erupted at once, some of it from Garcia's weapon, but Calderon was already up and moving by then, Rodriguez on his heels.

He cleared the threshold, turned right toward the stairwell access door, and traveled all of twenty feet before a bullet slammed between his shoulder blades and pitched him forward, facedown, on the carpet.

Calderon felt nothing.

That was bad, yet somehow comforting. He tried to move his arms, rise to his hands and knees to crawl away, but it proved impossible. That told him that the bullet must have clipped his spine. The sudden pressure in his chest, a sense of dreadful fullness, told him it had done more damage still.

Aznar would be furious, but there was nothing he could do about it now. Maybe some other time, when he caught up to Calderon in Hell.

I'll see you there, the shooter thought, and slowly closed his eyes.

JACK GRIMALDI KNEW THEY were ass deep in alligators when Bolan didn't respond to his radio call. It got worse when Keely Ross answered instead, nearly sobbing, "Oh, God! It's Johnny! Help me stop him!"

It was worse because Grimaldi didn't know exactly where they were. Somewhere inside the pall of battle smoke that screened the hallway from his view, presumably, but that didn't tell him a thing beyond the general direction he needed to travel.

He put it together on the move. Bolan was off the air, and his kid brother had done something wild enough to spook Ross at a level Grimaldi had yet to observe in the lady's repertoire of emotions.

Worst case scenario: Mack was down, maybe dead, and Johnny was rushing to join him. By now, they could both be casualties, maybe KIA.

That numbing thought kept Grimaldi in motion, let him chop down a pair of shooters who blocked his path without really thinking about it, pressing on toward the heart of the action.

What would he do if Bolan was dead? If they *both* were?

"Jack? Where are you?" Keely Ross called again.

"I'm headed your way. Call it thirty yards from the Russian's doorstep."

"I've lost Johnny. No, wait—there he is. He's—"

Gunfire smothered the rest of it and Grimaldi ducked lower as bullets flayed the wall above his head. So much for the five-star accommodations. Moving on, Grimaldi hugged the wall, duck-walking, tracking with his MP-5 in search of hostile targets.

Watch for Bolan. Watch for Johnny. Watch for Ross.

He found Johnny first, crouching over a dead man and shouting, "Where is he?" while shaking the limp form. Blood spattered from ugly head wounds, but with no pulse to spread it around.

Grimaldi knelt beside Johnny, unflinching as the kid's SA-80 swung up toward his face then retreated. "What's going on?" he asked.

"It's Mack," Johnny replied. "He's gone. They've taken him somewhere."

"You're sure? I mean—"

"He's gone! He'd answer, otherwise."

"He could be—"

"No! I would've found him. He's not dead. He's MIA."

"Okay. But this guy isn't talking anymore."

Johnny released the corpse and wiped his bloody palms on his trousers. "We have to find him."

"Find who?" Ross asked, coming through the haze to join them.

Johnny almost answered straight, then caught himself, remembering. "They've taken Matt," he said.

"No elevators, with the fire alarm," Grimaldi said. "That leaves one way out."

"Let's move!" Johnny commanded. He was up and running toward the service stairs before Grimaldi could respond.

Johnny hit the stairs running and slipped in a pool of tacky blood. He clutched at the rail—more blood here—it slipped wet through his fingers and he landed heavily on one hip, gasping at the sudden pain.

"Are you okay?" Grimaldi asked him, standing on the stairs above.

"I'm fine."

Johnny lurched to his feet, hobbling down the first few steps until his leg remembered how to function properly. His grip was firm on the SA-80, finger outside the trigger guard for safety's sake, but ready to fire the moment any member of the opposition showed himself.

Where were they? How far could they travel with their burden in such a short time?

Far enough, he decided, and put on more speed.

The hip was bruised, but nothing worse, as far as he could tell. He pushed on, ignoring the pain, one level after another, with Grimaldi and Ross close behind him.

Ten floors meant twenty flights. They no longer had the fire stairs to themselves, with frightened guests streaming down to the street, but their guns cleared the way for the most part.

The lobby was chaos, which helped with their cover but made spotting enemies more difficult. The trio held their weapons low, if not entirely out of sight, and moved into the human crush, searching. Despite the press and racket, Johnny only needed a minute and change to know that his brother was gone.

"They're not here," he told Ross and Grimaldi.

"You know what we have to do then," Grimaldi replied.

"It's not right," Johnny said.

"There's no choice! We can't go through the whole damned hotel with the fire brigade coming."

Johnny hesitated and felt Ross tugging his sleeve. "He's right," she said. "We need to go right now."

They went out through the service entrance and across the parking lot to the car. It took perhaps two minutes—but it was the longest walk of Johnny's life.

10

Pablo Aznar couldn't sleep. He'd expected a report from Calderon's hit team by 1:00 a.m., maybe 1:30 at the latest. If they failed in their mission, he had Bahamian detectives on the payroll who would call him from the crime scene with a briefing. Still, he'd heard nothing by 2:15, when he flipped on the television in his penthouse bedroom and turned to a twenty-four-hour news channel.

The lead story, in progress when Aznar tuned in, was a live report from the scene of a tragic hotel fire in Nassau. A stunning young reporter, black and beautiful, was talking to the camera with fire trucks and a long shot of a beachfront hotel in the background.

Breathlessly the woman told him, "Once again, there's no word on the cause of a deadly fire that swept through one floor of the Royal Nassau Hotel tonight. We have an unconfirmed report of explosions inside the hotel, but police refuse comment so far. The fire was apparently confined to the hotel's tenth floor, but we're told there are multiple fatalities. No victims have thus far been identified. Authorities say their investigation is continuing. As you can see...."

Aznar heard a telephone ringing somewhere beyond his bedroom door, and he muted the TV to wait for his houseman.

The silent images in front of him—bleary-eyed hotel guests in their robes and pajamas, firemen handling hoses the size of well-fed pythons—told Aznar what he already knew in his heart and in his gut.

The call could only be bad news.

A soft knock sounded on his door and Aznar said, "Come in."

The houseman held a cordless telephone in one hand, glancing briefly at the television as he crossed the room and handed it to Aznar.

"Who is it?" Aznar demanded.

"The Russian who was here this afternoon," the houseman answered.

Borodin? How could it be?

"Leave me."

Aznar sat waiting for the bedroom door to close, then keyed the phone and said, "Hello?"

"I hope I'm not upsetting someone's beauty sleep," said Semyon Borodin.

Aznar felt sour acid churning in his stomach. He couldn't read the Russian's tone. Was there a hint of mockery? Was Borodin fishing to see if Aznar was surprised to find him still alive?

He settled for a compromise. "Semyon? What do you want?" It was intended to sound gruff enough for someone who'd been roused from sleep, but without a ring of guilt.

"A place to stay," the Russian said. "It seems my hotel was a firetrap, and we've had to leave. You didn't hear the news, then?"

"No." A simple lie.

"Alas, there's been another incident," said Borodin. "We were attacked at the hotel, my friend."

"Attacked?" Aznar was careful not to overdo his simulation of surprise.

"Indeed. It's shocking, no?"

"But you're all right?"

"Some losses." He could almost see Borodin shrug, as if

his soldiers had no value in the scheme of things. "How do you feel about surprises, Pablo?"

Here it comes, thought Aznar. First the accusations, then the threats. "I don't know what you mean," he said, stalling.

"Only this. I've managed to do in one night what your over-priced mercenary couldn't do in two weeks."

"Meaning?"

"I've taken one of our enemies," Borodin gloated. "I have him. *Alive.*"

Aznar swallowed the sour taste of panic. If Borodin had captured one of Calderon's men—much less Guillermo himself—the Russian would soon know that Aznar had attempted to kill him. He might know already, playing out more rope to see if Aznar would tie his own noose.

Bluff it out, he thought. And said, "What has he told you?"

"Nothing yet," said Borodin. Lying? Was it a trap?

"You haven't questioned him?" Aznar could only hope his tone was casual.

"He's still unconscious from a head wound," the Russian explained. "I prefer him so, for the moment. As I said, we need a quiet place to stay and carry on the questioning without unnecessary interruptions."

It was time to make the offer. Borodin wouldn't accept if he had any reason to believe that Aznar was his enemy. "I have a place," said the Colombian. "It's safe, outside the city. I could meet you there."

Borodin hesitated just long enough to leave Aznar in doubt, then said, "By all means, I accept your hospitality."

Aznar allowed himself a measure of relief. If they were on his ground, inside his house, it couldn't be a trap. "If you need transportation—"

"No. The cars are still intact."

It was a hitch, but nothing major. "Good," Aznar replied. "I'll give you the directions, if you have a pen."

"I'm ready," answered Borodin.

And so am I, thought the Colombian as he began to speak once more.

JOHNNY WAS NUMB. He hadn't felt this way since the deaths of his parents and sister years before, when he was still an adolescent.

Mack's not dead, he told himself, but the curt reassurance rang hollow.

"What are we going to do?"

The question came from Keely Ross, riding shotgun with Grimaldi at the wheel. They had been cruising aimlessly for half an hour since their flight from Borodin's hotel, Johnny staring blankly out the window at shops and restaurants closed for the night.

Grimaldi echoed Johnny's thoughts. "First thing," he said, "we need to agree that he's probably still alive."

"How can you know that?" Ross inquired.

"Because they *took* him," Johnny said. "Borodin wouldn't leave his own men dead in the hotel and carry off a stranger's corpse. The only reason to take him is if he can talk."

"Interrogation, then." The lady's voice was grim.

"That's it."

"Which means we need to find him soon," Grimaldi said. He didn't have to add the whys and wherefores.

The pictures playing out in Johnny's head were bad enough without a soundtrack for narration.

"Find him, right," Ross said. "And how do we do that, again?"

"Okay." Grimaldi kept his eyes on the traffic as he spoke, charting an aimless course through downtown Nassau. "We were after Borodin tonight, so it's a natural assumption that the Russians made the snatch—except we weren't alone in there. We don't know who the other shooters were. And more importantly, we don't know which side carried off our guy."

"So, it's a toss-up, then?" Ross asked.

"That's right," Grimaldi said. "But one side of the coin is still blank. We could spend all night chasing Borodin, and blow the game because we should be after God knows who."

"You make it sound hopeless."

"Not yet," said Johnny, turning from the window to his friends. "We hit two fronts at once," he continued. "First thing, we know that someone local has a handle on the situation. Asking one guy or a hundred, I don't care. We work the field and rattle their cages until something develops."

"And two?" asked Grimaldi.

"Your guy in Washington," Johnny replied, omitting Brognola's name. "He always wants to help, so here's his chance."

"As in…?"

"He won't know where they're holding Matt, but he can likely point us toward the kinds of places where they might conduct interrogations. Any hard sites or retreats around Nassau, or within easy travel distance."

"It's worth a shot," Grimaldi granted.

"Okay. Then all we have to do is figure out who's first for Q and A."

Ross half turned in her seat to face him. "I'd say the Russians first, if we can find them. Play the odds. If nothing else, maybe they'll have a fix on who the other shooters were."

If we can find them, Johnny's mind echoed. And if we can't, then what?

Then he would question someone else, and someone after that, until he got the information he required.

"Makes sense," he said to Ross. "We play the odds to start and hope we're lucky for a change."

"Still," Grimaldi suggested, "finding Borodin after tonight could be a tricky proposition. We can't stroll into the cop shop and ask if they know where he's hiding."

"So maybe I should talk to the Colombians," Johnny replied. "It's their turf, after all."

"It's risky," Grimaldi reminded him.

"It is," Johnny granted as he turned back toward the window once again. "For them."

BEFORE ATTEMPTING TO follow Aznar's directions, Borodin ordered the limousine stopped for his soldiers to check on the bound passenger in the trunk. Borodin even got out and walked around behind the car to see the man himself.

The stranger was still unconscious, but the seepage of blood from his head wound had slackened and was beginning to clot in his hair. Borodin knew next to nothing about medicine, but he could tell the man was breathing, and that was enough for the moment.

"Close it up," he ordered, then retreated to his place inside the vehicle.

It didn't feel like luxury tonight, despite the car's accessories: a wet bar, satellite television, CD and DVD players, and a sunroof tinted nearly as dark as the car's jet-black paint job. Regardless of the ride, he was a fugitive, running and hiding from enemies still unidentified, and that feeling infuriated the Russian.

It had been years since Semyon Borodin had been forced to run from anyone, police and prosecutors included. He recalled the bad old days well enough to find them distasteful, and he vowed that someone would suffer for making him feel that way again.

Someone would pay, beginning with the stranger in his trunk.

Borodin had no idea who the gunman was, or who he represented, but the Russian meant to find out. Coming up from the streets, he'd learned methods of not-so-gentle persuasion that were ultimately irresistible. Borodin would keep the stranger alive until he had obtained the necessary information—all of it—and then he'd treat the bastard to a screaming death that would make the interrogation seem like a lover's caress by comparison.

But first, Borodin thought, he'd have to deal with the Colombians. Aznar had sounded different on the telephone when Borodin surprised him. It might have been something as simple as sleep, or maybe Borodin had caught him with a woman at the height of passion, but there'd been something....

Colombians were treacherous, like Turks and Chechens. Borodin dealt with them often, for cocaine and other contraband he couldn't get from any other source, but he had never trusted them.

Now, however, he was forced to wonder if there might be something more than simple shiftiness at work behind the scenes.

The raid on his hotel had been chaotic, not because his men were such able defenders, but rather because the first strike team had been interrupted by a second one. Borodin had trouble grasping that concept while he was caught in the midst of a fight for his life, but now that he was safe—for the moment, at least—he had time to assess the full import of the fact.

Two raiding parties meant two enemies, and one of them was almost certainly a fellow member of the Isla de Victoria cartel. The other, Borodin assumed, must represent the same unknown force that had trashed their operations in New Orleans, Miami and Panama City.

A false friend, he reckoned—but who?

Borodin had glimpsed one of the original raiders before his soldiers had moved in and cut the man down. He hadn't been Asian, but that didn't rule out a murder contract arranged by Sun or Tanaka. By the same token, Borodin couldn't think how he might have offended either the Yakuza or the White Lotus Triad Society.

At least, not recently.

If the Asians hadn't tried to kill him, that left the Colombians or the Sicilians. Either group was capable of ruthless action, clearly—but again, Borodin wasn't sure why they would try to take him out tonight, when there had been so many other opportunities.

If Aznar was to blame for the attack, Borodin was playing directly into his hands by seeking refuge at the Colombian's safe house. On the other hand, if the Ambrosio family had placed a price on his head, the men from Medellin could be useful allies, for a price.

There was, of course, one other possibility.

Borodin had made no secret of his feelings toward Garrett Tripp. The mercenary knew it, and his military training might dictate the wisdom of a swift preemptive strike. If so, it was unlikely that he'd cleared it with the others first. Borodin's allies had too much at stake to side with the hired help against one of their strongest partners.

And yet...

Because he wasn't absolutely sure, couldn't be sure beyond the shadow of a nagging doubt, it would be all the more imperative to grill his prisoner and so identify the other enemy. That information, Borodin reasoned, would make him valuable to the others. If he had an enemy in the cartel, that foe might reconsider any further moves once Borodin had proved himself an asset to the team.

So, answers first.

And then revenge.

The Russian would have both, he vowed. And when the time was right, he'd wash his hands in the blood of all those who defied him.

HANDCUFFS.

He recognized the feel of them, a not-to-be-forgotten chill of stainless steel on flesh, sharp-edged enough to draw blood if he fought them, tight enough to leave his fingertips tingling from reduced circulation.

Once you've worn handcuffs, they'll never be mistaken for any other kind of restraint—rawhide thongs or loops of baling wire. There's a professional feel to handcuffs. You know they mean business.

Bolan knew testing the bracelets was most probably a waste of time but he did it anyway. Flexing his wrists confirmed that there was no play in the cuffs, and a bit of finger play assured him that his hands had been secured back-to-back, thus defeating any scheme to tamper with the manacles.

It was a professional job.

He was stuck with it.

Stuck in a car trunk, a mode of transportation as unmistakable as the steel clamps on his wrists. It was fairly spacious, as such accommodations went, but there was no escaping the mingled odors of rubber, grease and exhaust fumes.

The smell exacerbated Bolan's headache, already a throbbing ass kicker without any help from an olfactory accomplice. He recalled the last conscious moments of his battle outside Semyon Borodin's hotel suite—no short-term amnesia, at least—and guessed that shrapnel or debris from his own frag grenade had delivered the knockout punch. Less concerned with irony than survival, he dismissed that information from his mind and focused on the questions that might determine his fate.

Who were his captors?

And where the hell were they taking him?

The rumble at Borodin's hotel had been a three-sided fight, with unknown shooters on the Russian's case before Bolan's team joined the party. Bolan didn't know which side had captured him. Borodin would have been forced to evacuate the hotel after the fireworks show, and the attackers—those who had survived—would likewise seek to flee before police surrounded the establishment.

No answer as to who, then, but they clearly wanted him alive. If not, they'd have put a bullet in his throbbing head and spared themselves the risk of hauling him all over Nassau.

Were they even still in Nassau?

Bolan's sense of time was off. He couldn't check his watch and, in the circumstances, Bolan found he couldn't judge time's passage by the crust of blood around his wound. It simply hurt like Hell, with no distinction between laceration and bruising.

Live capture meant they wanted something from him and smart money said that would be information, for starters. They'd want to know who he was, who he worked for, the names and location of any companions in Nassau. If they found a safe place to interrogate him, Bolan took for granted that they'd ultimately break him down. No one could beat interrogation in the long run, when the gloves came off and there were no holds barred. It was not a matter of *if* he would crack, but *when* it would happen.

Unless…

There were two ways to cheat the inquisitors. One was to escape, but Bolan couldn't judge the odds of a successful getaway in his present position. He could only wait and be prepared to act if an opportunity presented itself.

The other cheat hatch was death.

It wasn't the option he favored, but it was still preferable to days of screaming agony with no rescue in sight. Far better, in Bolan's mind, than betraying his friends and the Stony Man team.

Something to think about, at least.

As the car rolled on, bewildering Bolan with its twists and turns, the prisoner knew that his options finally came down to only one.

For freedom, for his friends, for a release from pain, Bolan would kill—either his captors or himself. Time and circumstance would determine the ultimate choice.

Right now, there was nothing that the Executioner could do but bide his time and wait.

Arlington, Virginia

HAL BROGNOLA TOOK the call at home, drawn from the misty threshold of sleep by the insistent trilling of the cordless telephone beside his bed. He kept the ringer's volume turned down low, a courtesy to his wife, but in fact she'd learned to live with late-night calls and barely noticed anymore. Perhaps the ringing telephone intruded on her dreams and sent them spinning in a new direction. Brognola couldn't say.

He palmed the phone, already up and moving toward the bathroom as he spoke. "It's your dime. Talk to me."

"We've got a problem," Johnny Gray replied.

Brognola stepped into the bathroom and shut the door. It was pitch-black without the lights, as he leaned back against the sink. "What's that?"

"Mack's gone," the kid explained. "The opposition grabbed him."

A sudden wave of vertigo sent Brognola groping for the light switch. The glare hurt his eyes, but it put him back in the here-and-now world and so kept him from falling.

"What?"

"You heard me right. We lost him, Hal."

Jesus. "Is he… I mean…"

"We don't have any answers," Johnny said. "That's why I'm calling you."

"Okay. Can you at least tell me what happened?"

"We went after Borodin. It was supposed to be a change of pace, throw off the opposition, maybe shake some information loose. It sounded like a good idea."

"Okay."

"Someone was there ahead of us, at Borodin's hotel. Shooters. I don't know who or why. We mixed it up and…something happened. Mack broke contact. When we swept the place…he wasn't there."

"You think they took him out?" Brognola instantly regretted the choice of words, but Johnny seemed to miss it.

"I'm pretty sure."

"You checked the rooms?"

"Some of them," Johnny hedged. "There wasn't time to cover everything. The place was burning and the cops were rolling in. Nobody stuck around the tenth floor unless—"

Unless they were dead, Brognola silently finished for him, guessing the kid couldn't say it. Not yet.

There were other takes, of course. Bolan could've been knocked unconscious or wounded, his communications gear disabled. If he'd been grabbed, the snatch team might've gone to ground on another floor of the hotel, hoping to wait out the fire alarm and slip away later.

There were options galore—but he trusted Johnny's gut instinct.

"How can I help?" Brognola asked.

"We're going to be shaking up some people here, looking for leads, but it would help to get a fix on any safe houses or hard sites in the neighborhood, if they're on file. From what I understand about the local situation, I suppose that means Colombians, primarily."

"Aznar and Santiago, right."

"So, if they've got someplace besides the hotel where Aznar's been hanging out—"

"I'll make a call," Brognola said. "You have the same cell phone?"

"Affirmative."

It could've been the older brother's voice, Brognola thought—except it wasn't. It might never be again.

"I'll see what's in the system and get back to you ASAP, whichever way it goes."

"Appreciate it," Johnny said.

"Don't count him out, okay? Not yet."

"I won't." The younger Bolan's voice was frosting over as he spoke. "But if it goes that way, you'll want to brief the DEA and anybody else to get their undercover people clear."

"I'll handle it."

Brognola didn't have to ask what Johnny meant. If he discovered that his brother had been sacrificed, there'd be no mercy for the men responsible or any of their hangers-on.

Scorched earth.

He broke the link to Nassau and tapped out the number for Stony Man Farm, praying as he dialed that it was not already too late.

"YOU MISSED HIM?" Hector Santiago's voice was calm. He did not rant or shout. He trusted Pablo Aznar to feel his displeasure in spite of the distance between them.

"I'm sorry, yes." Aznar must truly be intimidated if he felt compelled to offer an apology.

That thought almost made Santiago smile. Instead he sipped his drink, listened to the ice cubes clash softly in the sweaty glass, and said, "He got away. Escaped completely, after all your planning."

"Yes, sir. But that's not—"

"What of the men you sent?"

Aznar would know that there was nothing to be gained from hesitation. "Dead," he instantly replied.

"How many?"

"Nine. But—"

"Nine men dead." Santiago stressed the number as if it meant something. "Can they be identified?"

"I don't think so," Aznar replied.

"You don't *think* so?"

"Hector, there's more important news."

"More important than Borodin killing my men and escaping unscathed? By all means, tell me, Pablo. I can't wait to hear it."

"He doesn't know we staged the raid," Aznar began.

"Go on, then. I'm listening." Another sip, the liquor sliding down his throat. Chilled fire.

"Another hit team tried for Borodin at the same time," Aznar continued. "I believe they were the same ones from Panama City, maybe the same from Miami."

"So they killed my men?"

"Forget about the dead men for a minute, will you? Borodin *caught* one of them."

"One of the others?"

"That's what I'm telling you."

"Caught him alive?

"Alive. We mean to question him and find out who he's working for."

"When you say 'we,' you mean…"

"Myself and Borodin."

"You're friends again?"

"*Still* friends," Aznar replied. "I promise you, he doesn't know we tried to take him out."

"I hope not, Pablo, for your sake."

That forced Aznar to pause before he asked, "What do you mean?"

"Only the obvious. "He's there in Nassau, where you are. I take it that he plans to join you—when?"

"He's on his way out to the country house. I'll join him there."

"And any soldiers he has left."

"I know this one," Aznar declared. "Don't worry."

"I'm not worried, Pablo," Santiago answered. "I'm safe at home in Medellin."

"Of course." There was an angry stiffness in Aznar's tone, telling Santiago he'd scored with his barb.

"Have you considered moving the prisoner?" Santiago asked.

"I told you, Borodin's moving him now."

"I mean, out of the country, Pablo."

"Where would we take him?"

Santiago sighed, closing his eyes. "Someplace where you control the odds, without relying on a pack of foreigners."

"You mean, bring him to Medellin?"

"I simply offer it as food for thought. The hunters are in Nassau. Unless I'm very much mistaken, they'll be looking for him as we speak. I know *I* would be."

"I'll talk to Borodin."

"You have my every confidence. Be careful, eh, Pablo?"

Santiago broke the connection before Aznar had a chance to respond. Leave him nervous and guessing, feeling the pressure to prove himself anew after the latest failure. Edgy subordinates were the best kind, in Santiago's view. Complacent men were sluggish and useless.

If Aznar succeeded in delivering the prisoner, he would have performed a valuable service. If he failed...well, there were always more where Pablo came from, eager young men lined up and waiting for their shot at the Big Time.

If Aznar had to be replaced for any reason, it could be the qualifying test. In fact, Santiago decided, he might as well start drawing up a list of prospects for the job. It would be entertaining, and should help him pass the time until he faced his enemies.

Because they would be coming for the captive. Santiago had no doubt of that.

In fact, he was counting on it.

AGAINST ALL ODDS, Bolan was dozing when the vehicle reached its destination. He registered the cessation of movement and came back to consciousness, groggy and hurting.

There'd been a dream of sorts, dark and bloody, but the details now eluded him.

Just as well, he thought.

Waking reality was grim enough.

He heard and felt the car doors slamming, registered a sound of footsteps on gravel as someone walked around behind the car to fetch him. Bolan closed his eyes and focused on relaxing, trying to adopt the slack posture of unconsciousness that so few actors can achieve.

He didn't know where they were or what would happen next, but there was no point in burning up precious energy if he could avoid it, especially in his weakened state. He'd make the bastards carry him, if possible.

The trunk lid opened. Bolan willed his eyelids not to flicker as a light came on inside his hidey-hole. Above him, gruff male voices spoke incomprehensible words. Bolan first thought the blow to his head had scrambled something inside, then he realized the language wasn't English. Something from the Balkans, maybe.

Russian?

But it was English the next time one of them spoke. Rough-edged and heavily accented, but English all the same.

"You still alive in there?" one of them asked.

"I see him breathe," another said.

"Don't think I want to carry that big fucker," said the first.

"Wake up!" the second voice commanded, followed by a round of laughter from several men.

Bolan knew he could play it out further, maybe compel them to prod or punch him where he lay, but what was the point? Why should he invite more injury without benefit to himself, before he had even sized up his options?

He cracked an eye, surveying his captors. Four beefy men were lined up, peering into the trunk. None of them resembled the mug shots of Semyon Borodin.

"What happened?" he asked them, sounding slightly weaker than he felt. "Where am I?"

"Questions he's got," one of the Russians said. "You don't ask questions, son of bitch. You answer."

"Get out of the trunk," another Russian ordered.

Bolan made a show of rocking back and forth without real progress. "I can't move my arms," he said.

"You goddamned right," said the first man who had spoken.

Bolan began to worm his way around, stretching his legs by slow degrees and extending them over the lip of the trunk. "I'm not sure I can do this," he told them. Only a part of his grimace was feigned.

"Too slow," the first one said, and nodded to a pair of flankers. The others leaned in and grabbed Bolan, one by each manacled arm, and hoisted him out of the trunk. His scalp grazed the lid in passing, and a fresh wave of pain made the world tilt crazily as they set him on his feet.

"Watch there!" the man in charge commanded, and the lifters held Bolan upright while he swayed in their grasp. He managed not to vomit, but it took most of his willpower.

"Better," the crew chief said. "Now come and meet the man you try to kill."

Sandwiched between his captors, Bolan moved along a curving gravel driveway toward a house that bulked up large and ominous, like a fortress in the dark.

11

"What's the word from Washington?" Grimaldi asked as soon as Johnny closed the door behind him.

"They'll get back to me," Johnny replied. "Safe houses, hard sites, anything like that, they'll try to pin it down."

"Could work," Grimaldi said. He sounded skeptical.

"It won't be fast enough," Johnny replied. "For all we know, they're working on him right this minute."

"Maybe not," said Keely Ross. "If we assume they'll take him out of town, that buys some time."

"Not much."

"Okay," she countered. "But we can't do anything about it sitting here. So what's the plan?"

They'd already discussed the broad strokes, but Johnny had worked out some of the details during his run to call Brognola. He laid it out now, as succinctly as possible, remembering to use his brother's code name for Ross's sake.

"Here it is," he declared. "We were after Borodin when Matt went missing, so we know one side of the equation, Russians. The other side's an unknown variable and there's nothing we can do about it for the moment. We can only work with what we have."

"We want a Russki, then," Grimaldi said.

"As close to Borodin as possible," Johnny confirmed.

Ross interjected. "Suppose the Russians don't have Matt. What then? How can they help us if the other guys made off with him?"

"Maybe they can't," Johnny replied. "But there's a chance they recognized the other shooters and can tell us who they were, who sent them, something. Anything. If they don't know, I guarantee they're pulling out the stops and trying every trick they know to pin an ID on the hit team. If we catch a lucky break, maybe they'll do the work and we can reap the benefits."

"It could work," Ross admitted.

"Plus, there's one more thing," he added. "If I don't get out of here soon and do something, I'm going to lose what's left of my mind."

"I hear that," Grimaldi echoed.

"Okay," Ross said. "Where do we start? I mean, with Borodin flushed out of the hotel and running who knows where, how do we find one of his people to interrogate?"

"We had a list of targets going in," Johnny reminded her. He raised a hand and tapped his temple with his index finger. "I've still got it filed up here."

"You think it's accurate, after tonight? Business as usual, with their goombah running for his life?" Ross asked.

"I'll settle for stragglers, if that's all we can find. The other choice is sitting here and knowing we did nothing while the pricks were taking Matt apart."

Ross paled at that, breaking eye contact with Johnny. "You know I didn't mean that. I'm just thinking, if we run off willy-nilly chasing shadows, it could make things worse."

"Matt's head is on the block," Grimaldi said. "It can't get any worse."

"We've been through this before," Johnny advised. "Rattling cages works, most of the time."

"What do you mean?" Ross asked, eyes flicking back and

forth from one man to the other. "Are you telling me Matt has been captured before?"

"Not Matt." Johnny frowned, thinking back to another time, another battleground. "Last time, it was me in the bag."

"My God! I didn't…you never… What happened?"

Johnny shrugged. "I'm here, right? Matt did what he had to do, and I'm alive."

"Okay. I have to ask you, though," she said.

He knew the question in advance and was ready for it. "Go ahead."

"Suppose he *isn't*. Still alive, I mean. What, then?"

"Same game," Johnny replied, "with fewer players. We make up the shortage with ferocity. Scorched earth."

"I see."

"You up for that?" he asked her.

For a moment Johnny found himself hoping she'd bow out, go back home and let him finish out the game with Jack Grimaldi. Silently, he willed her to reject the mission, let it go. He hoped she would choose life.

He lost that hope, as Ross smiled.

"Why not?" she said. "It's not like I have anywhere to be, right? Count me in."

"Perfect," Grimaldi said. "Now all we need to do is find a mark."

"I've got a fair idea where we can look," said Johnny, rising from his chair. "Let's go."

No MATTER WHERE HE WENT, Grimaldi found that waterfronts were pretty much the same. An island tourist site like Nassau might have two, one of them squeaky clean for yachts and cruise ships, while the other would resemble any dock he'd ever seen from Singapore to San Diego. It had greasy pilings, sleazy bars where sailors could get lucky for a price, pawn shops and tattoo parlors in place of stylish boutiques.

And this night, Grimaldi hoped, it would have at least one Russian mobster on the prowl.

Borodin's crime family had established a beachhead on Nassau several years earlier, according to intelligence from Stony Man. They hadn't challenged Santiago's primacy in the Bahamas, but the islands had a live-and-let-live attitude where illicit enterprises were concerned. The police and politicians were equal-opportunity grifters, as happy with rubles as they were with dollars, yen or pesos.

Borodin's place on the docks was a foothold, nothing more, though it had expanded since he'd joined forces with Santiago and the rest to back Maxwell Reed as the next Caribbean strong man. The operations specialized in short-term loans with long-term consequences for borrowers who couldn't pay. They operated from a tiny office set above a massage parlor called Squeeze Play. Lights were burning in the office when Grimaldi parked the rental on the street below.

"Somebody's home," he said.

"Night watchman," Ross suggested.

"It's a start," Johnny replied. "I'll take what I can get."

"There could be more than one," Grimaldi said, "if they're expecting trouble."

"Right." Johnny cradled an MP-5 in his lap, watching the loan shark's lighted windows from the shotgun seat, "I'd better go and see."

"Let me," Ross offered.

"What?"

"You go up there, all macho-looking in the middle of the night, Borodin's people will probably shoot you on sight. I, on the other hand, have an advantage."

"What's that?" Grimaldi asked.

"I'm just your basic damsel in distress. I'm lost, my car died, and I'm feeling helpless. What's a girl to do?"

"These people, I don't know," Johnny replied.

"They might decide to throw a party in your honor," said Grimaldi. "You could be the cake and ice cream."

"In which case," she answered, flashing her SIG-Sauer P-226, "I'll just have to blow out the candles. Don't worry, though. I'll save you one."

"You can't go in alone," Johnny said, and swiveled in his seat to stare at her.

"Alone's the only way that works," Ross said.

"She's right," Grimaldi interjected. "You can't run a damsel-in-distress scenario if she's already got a man on tap."

"I still don't like it," Johnny said.

"What's the alternative?" Ross asked. "You want to go in through the front door, shooting anything that moves? Who'll be your source when they're all dead?"

"Okay, I get the point. We need to have you covered, though."

"Sounds fair," Ross said. "Let's do this thing."

"Where's that leave me?" Grimaldi asked.

"On tap to get us out of here," said Johnny, "if it blows up in our faces."

Grimaldi sat and watched them cross the street together, Johnny stopping at the bottom of the outside stairs while Ross went up and knocked. It took a while for anyone to answer, but the door finally opened, framing Ross in a pale shaft of light. Grimaldi watched her check out the room beyond the threshold, wishing he could see it through her eyes. The pistol in his hand felt heavy, almost sentient, anxious to slice off a piece of the action.

After another long moment Ross pointed down toward the street. A man joined her on the upstairs landing, more intent on ogling her body than checking out her ride. He said something, Ross responded with a smile, and then the guy reached out a hand, as if to cup her breast.

It was his first and last mistake.

Grimaldi missed the punch, it was that fast, but he saw the Russian come tumbling downstairs like an acrobat long out of practice. Johnny was there when the mark touched down in a heap, dragging the Russian to his feet before he had time to recoup from the fall.

Grimaldi had the engine running, ready for them, as Johnny and Ross quick-marched their prisoner across the street and shoved him into the back seat.

GREGORI ROSTOV KNEW he was in trouble. What he didn't know was how serious that trouble might prove to be—and whether he would survive it.

His captors didn't attempt to hide where they were taking him. Rostov took that as a bad sign, indicating they had no fear of reprisals because he wouldn't be alive to carry tales.

So far, they'd said nothing beyond curt instructions to keep his mouth shut. Rostov's hands were tightly bound behind his back. They'd taken his pistol and the woman had it pointed at his groin now, holding the weapon as if she knew well how to use it. One shot at that range would emasculate him, but Rostov thought he might risk it, if it seemed they were about to kill him.

He was still alive, though, and perhaps he could stay that way yet, if he was able to appease these crazy people without betraying Semyon Borodin.

How much could he reveal, without incurring Borodin's colossal wrath?

It was a tightrope act, Rostov realized, and a fall in either direction would be fatal.

The driver stopped and killed the engine. Rostov's captors piled out of the car and ordered him to follow them. The pistol, zeroed on his crotch like a compass needle seeking true north, persuaded him to comply without argument.

"YOU WOULD HAVE KILLED him," Keely Ross remarked when they were two blocks from the hospital.

"I should have," Johnny said, "but he's my messenger to Borodin."

Ross turned away and watched the first faint light of dawn breaking to eastward, behind Nassau's skyline.

"I didn't know it would be like this," she said. "Brutality, torture—and for what? We still don't know where Matt is."

"But we know who has him," Johnny replied. There was no anger in his voice, but weariness had crept into it.

And he was right. Ross had to grant him that. Their prisoner had drawn the line at losing both kneecaps. He'd confirmed a second-hand report that Semyon Borodin had bagged a prisoner during the hotel firefight, and that Borodin hoped to gain crucial intelligence from the captive before they disposed of him. Unfortunately, their informant was too far down the food chain to know where Borodin had taken his prisoner, and the mobster he'd suggested as a source of further information—one Nicolai Yurochka—had fled the Royal Nassau Hotel with his boss, leaving no forwarding address.

Johnny had left the Russian with a message when they dropped him off curbside, half a block from the entrance to an emergency ward. It had been short and easy to remember, even for a man in grievous pain.

"Tell Borodin I'm coming. There's no place to hide."

Except there was, apparently, because they still had no idea where they could find the Russian or retrieve their leader. All they'd done tonight, as far as Ross could tell, was give one thug a limp and warn their enemy that he should burrow deeper underground.

"I hope your guy in Washington comes up with something soon," she said.

"I hope so, too," Johnny answered. "Because we're running out of time."

"YOU WANT US TO GO *where?*"

Aznar was prepared for the Russian's attitude—suspicion, anger, worry, as if negative emotions had been churned up in a blender to create the perfect aggravation cocktail. What he hadn't seen, so far, was any indication that the Russian knew Aznar's gunmen had tried to kill him only hours earlier.

"It wasn't my idea, you understand," Aznar replied. He was the very picture of conciliation, reasonable to a fault. "Señor Santiago suggested that you and your men might be more comfortable in Medellin, where your security is guaranteed."

"You guaranteed it here," the Russian answered, sneering. "*This* was your refuge, your sanctuary after Panama."

"And I apologize for the disruption. It was unforeseen." The words left Aznar with a sour taste in his mouth.

"Oh, well, if you apologize, no doubt the men I've lost will all rest easy in their graves."

'I've told you—"

"I want Tripp," said Borodin. "He's fresh out of excuses now. I only voted to retain him at the last meeting because you all assured me there'd be no more lapses in security."

Aznar could not explain that *he* had breached security at Borodin's hotel. Instead he told the Russian, "Tripp will be here soon."

"And when he comes?"

"Before we get to that, let's talk about our prisoner."

"You mean to say my prisoner," said Borodin, correcting him.

"Semantics," the Colombian replied. "We're all still partners, are we not? He's damaged all of us. The information in his head may well be crucial to our undertaking. He belongs to all of us."

"And Santiago wants him tucked away in Medellin."

"For safety's sake," Aznar replied. "Señor Santiago is a businessman who looks after his interests and those of his friends. We are still friends, I take it?"

Instead of rising to the bait, Borodin said, "We have another matter to discuss, before the prisoner."

"You mean, the other men at your hotel."

"Exactly. It was obvious they didn't know each other. They were enemies, in fact. It's chiefly due to their reaction, killing one another, that I managed to escape."

"I can't explain it," Aznar said. "Unless…"

"Go on," said Borodin.

Aznar shrugged. "We all have enemies. This business we're in, it's inevitable. Perhaps some of yours—"

"What?" Borodin interrupted. "You think some enemies of mine from Russia followed me to a hotel in the Bahamas that I never heard of until yesterday? You think they came for me tonight and ran into another hit team by coincidence? Maybe the ones from Panama? Is that your brilliant explanation?"

In fact, it was the best Aznar could offer without telling the truth. Guilty as he was, Borodin's tone still offended him, but Aznar took pains not to show it.

"In any case," he offered, "we still think that you'll be safe in Medellin. I've made the same recommendation to all our associates."

"And the prisoner?"

"He would go with us, of course. In Medellin there are doctors—surgeons, psychiatrists—who specialize in drawing information from reluctant sources."

"And if I refuse?" asked Borodin.

"The choice is yours," Aznar replied. "You're free to come and go as you desire. We simply can't protect you while you're on your own."

Borodin frowned and said, "I haven't been to Medellin in years. The police were…unfriendly."

"Have no fear," said Aznar, smiling. "Everything will be arranged."

"In that case, I accept your hospitality—for now."

"For now," Aznar responded. Thinking, *Now is all I need.*

Arlington, Virginia

WHEN HAL BROGNOLA dialed Johnny's number, his call was answered on the second ring. A wary voice he recognized at once said, "Hello?"

"It's me," Brognola said. No names, as usual. "I've got that information you requested."

"Shoot."

"The home boys out of Medellin have got a place two miles outside Nassau. Aznar mostly uses it, but Santiago has been known to stay there on the odd occasion."

"Directions?" Johnny prodded.

"South of town, the main highway along the coastline," said Brognola. "Your target has a private beach, but the house is set back from the water a good hundred yards. Storm insurance, I guess. Ground access is a private road, connected to the highway. There's a sign, if you can believe it. Some old Colonial type called the place Shangri-La, way back when, and Santiago's crowd never got around to taking down the placard."

"Do we have a layout?" Johnny asked him. "Floor plans? Any aerials?"

"The DEA shoots bird's-eye views a couple of times a year. I got the latest batch from Stony Man. You want a fax or Jpeg file?"

"Jpegs are better." Johnny rattled off his laptop's e-mail address and Hal wrote it down.

"They're on the way," he told the kid. "If you need anything else…"

"Just time," Johnny said. "Can you arrange that for me?"

"If you need backup—" Brognola offered.

"No. They'd never make it here in time. We need to move on this."

"Your call. But if you need them later—"

"I won't hesitate to ask you."

That wasn't true, of course. If Johnny found his brother dead, there'd be no later. It would all come down to bloody action in the here and now.

Brognola wondered if Johnny would walk away from that one, if he'd even try. The Bolan brothers didn't spend a lot of time together, but they shared a bond that few others would ever know. And if that bond was severed...

He didn't want to think about it, couldn't think about it now. Instead of dwelling on the possibilities, he said, "Okay, then. You know where to reach me."

"Right."

Johnny was anxious to be gone. Brognola didn't hold him back. "Good luck," he said, and let the younger Bolan go.

That helpless feeling came back as he cradled the receiver.

BOLAN HEARD HIS CAPTORS coming. Even with the ringing in his ears, an echo from the head wound, he had no trouble making out the sound of footsteps in the corridor outside his cell.

The room where they'd confined him measured roughly eight by ten. Bolan had seen the whole thing when he entered, but half of it had been lost to him after his jailers had cuffed him to a straight-backed wooden chair, facing the door.

The chair wasn't bolted to the floor. He could have rocked it with his weight, or tipped it over, but that would only send him crashing down, increase the throbbing pain inside his head and maybe twist a shoulder out of joint. Bolan thought that with greater effort he could have worked the chair around to give himself a different view, but what would be the point?

He knew there were no other exits, no views preferable to the one that would let him watch his adversaries when they entered. The Executioner couldn't rise and face them, couldn't fight while he was cuffed, but he could read their faces, maybe judge what lay in store for him before they went to work.

There'd be no great surprises, he supposed. The bottom line with torture was inflicting pain, and there were only so many sensations that the human nervous system could transmit. Sharp pains, dull aches, a range of hot and cold in varying degrees. The options of a sadist were constrained by physiology.

They hadn't stripped him yet. And while Bolan couldn't be sure if that was by design or through some oversight, it came as a relief. It bought him time, if only seconds.

He wasn't counting on escape, but if he had a chance to kill one of his enemies, force them to use their guns...

A key turned in the lock and Bolan watched the door swing open. Semyon Borodin came in behind a bodyguard, two more crowding the room behind him. Bolan watched the Russian.

"I regret we haven't had more time together," Borodin declared, as if Bolan had been a weekend houseguest rather than a prisoner. "There are so many things we need to talk about."

"I've got nothing to say," the Executioner replied.

"Of course not." Borodin allowed himself a smile. "But you might reconsider, with the right inducement."

"Take your shot."

"I will...but not just now."

Bolan made no reply to that. Waiting.

"We're going to be traveling again, the two of us," said Borodin. The smile was full-blown now. "In fact, you're going where your friends will never find you and no one can hear you scream."

12

The DEA aerial photos gave Johnny Gray's team a feel for the target and had allowed them to rehearse their moves. Even knowing that it wouldn't be the same once they were on the ground and opposition was deployed, it was a bonus. The team was ready, though. As ready as they'd ever be.

The stakes had never been this high before, from Johnny's point of view. He'd fought for individuals, for countries, and for such abstract terms as liberty and justice, but they didn't measure up.

This time he would be fighting for his family.

Or what was left of it.

In war, you go for broke. The three remaining team members were dressed in tiger-striped fatigues, their hands and faces painted to take full advantage of the wooded grounds. A daylight probe was doubly risky, but they couldn't give the enemy any time to work on Mack—not if they wanted to bring him back alive, in any form resembling a human being.

Johnny was carrying their last SA-80 and the usual accessories, while Grimaldi and Ross packed MP-5s. They had divided their ammunition and grenades into fairly equal loads and brought it all along, in case they met more opposition than anticipated.

That would be a problem, Johnny realized. A photograph is out of date the instant the camera shutter snaps closed—and his DEA photos of the Colombian hard site were nearly four months old. He had no reason to believe they'd changed the layout in the meantime, but the snapshots couldn't tell him how many sentries were prowling the grounds or whether they'd been reinforced since last night.

Smart money said that if Bolan's captors had him caged on the estate, he would be under heavy guard. That meant a bitter fight to reach him, and the risk he'd be executed when they made their move.

Unless he was already dead.

Johnny derailed that train of thought before it left the station, concentrating on the moment. They were huddled in the shadow of a six-foot wall that surrounded the Colombian estate. According to the DEA report, there'd been no visible security devices three months earlier—which simply meant no razor wire, no broken glass and nails embedded in concrete atop the wall, no video surveillance cameras positioned so that passing motorists could see them from the road. Inside, there could be anything from rabid wolves to Claymore mines, and spotters passing by would never know.

"Last chance to bail," he told his two companions. "No hard feelings, either way."

"We're wasting time," Grimaldi said.

Ross nodded once. "Let's roll."

The wall was easy. Johnny scrambled over first then Jack gave Ross a boost and followed her over the top. Inside the wall, they crouched in dappled shadow for a moment. Waiting. Listening.

No dogs. No sirens. No troops rushing toward the wall.

So far.

"Okay," Johnny said. "We've run the drill. Let's find out how it works for real."

Silent nods all around before Johnny moved forward, due south toward the manor house, while Ross and Grimaldi jogged off east and west, flanking his line of march. With luck, they would all reach the target about the same time—assuming they reached it at all.

The house was barely visible, its roof line showing through trees that had been planted long ago. Each tree was a potential hiding place for enemies. Trip wires and other booby traps were not unthinkable.

But nearly halfway to the house, Johnny had met no opposition. He was starting to feel better bit by bit.

That's when the first shot sounded and it all went to Hell.

GARRETT TRIPP WAS HALFWAY through a mediocre breakfast when the shooting started. He'd been trying to enjoy it, after working through the night to beef up Pablo Aznar's personal security, but simple pleasure clearly wasn't in the cards.

The first round was a shotgun blast, which told him one of the Colombians had started it. Someday, Tripp thought, the trigger-happy bastards would unload on one another and the world would be a better place for it.

There'd been no warning from the walkie-talkie resting on the table, inches from his breakfast plate. Tripp raised it now and thumbed the red transmitter button. "What's that firing, dammit?" he demanded. "Talk to me!"

The voice of Perry Blake, his on-site Number Two, came back at Tripp. "I'm checking on it, sir. It's in the southern quadrant. There was no alert. I don't— Oh, shit!"

The radio went dead, the transmission interrupted by a burst of automatic fire. Tripp bolted from the table, barking orders even as he stooped to lift his Uzi submachine gun from the chair on his right.

"Watchman One, report!" Blake didn't answer to his code name—didn't answer, period—so Tripp revised his method.

"All points, talk to me. I want to know who's shooting, and I mean right now!"

Aznar was waiting in the foyer when Tripp got there, opening his mouth to speak, but Tripp ignored him as the walkie-talkie sounded.

"Watchman Three, sir. Nothing on the east, so far. I'll go and see what's happening with Watchman One. Over."

"That's negative! Stay at your post until I tell you otherwise. Confirm!"

"Affirmative," the disappointed voice came back.

"Watchman Two on station. The natives are restless."

"Keep them with you," Tripp ordered.

"Yes, sir!"

"Watchman Four. I can't control these bastards, sir, unless I—"

"Do it and leave this channel clear!"

Aznar was trailing him, demanding Tripp's attention. "Can you explain what's happening? Is that too much to ask?"

Tripp, still rapidly proceeding toward the nearest outside door, answered, "Sounds like one of your men ignored direct orders and started shooting," he told Aznar. "God knows why. They have the discipline of hyperactive children. Now I've got one station compromised, with contact broken, and your goons are going ape shit on the grounds. You want to join me, maybe we can get this cluster fuck cleared up and squared away. If all you want is conversation, it'll have to wait."

Tripp left the Colombian gaping, furious, as he made his way outside. He had more important things to think about at the moment than Pablo Aznar's temper. If the Colombian wanted to hassle him later, so be it. If Aznar got in his way while the bullets were flying—well, it wouldn't be the first time friendly fire took out a ranking officer.

It was a clear, warm morning, promising a sweaty afternoon. Tripp listened to the sounds of gunfire spreading across the southern quadrant of the property and scowled.

Goddamned Colombians!

They were ideal for cowboy jobs that called for them to roll in shooting, slaughter anything that moved, then take off in a cloud of dust and gunsmoke. Anything beyond that, though— even the simplest turn on lookout duty—strained their patience to the breaking point and left them itching for a fight. Most of the ones Tripp had been forced to deal with had a gnat's attention span, except where booze and women were concerned. They jumped at shadows and were never shy about unloading with the nearest weapon, on a whim.

The first grenade blast changed his mind. Tripp hadn't issued hand grenades to his men on the grounds and, as far as he knew, the Colombians carried only small arms.

Which meant trouble, now, with a capital T.

Tripp cursed and sprinted for the nearest corner of the house, racing to meet the enemy.

THE SHOOTER TOOK Grimaldi by surprise, or maybe it was mutual. Approaching through the trees in daylight, even with the camouflage fatigues and war paint, Jack felt like a sitting duck. He'd rather have been swooping down with the sun at his back, unloading on the big house with a 20 mm Gatling gun and Hellfire rockets, but the sledgehammer approach would be disastrous if the heavies had Bolan stashed on the grounds.

Distracted by such thoughts, if only for a microsecond, Grimaldi almost missed the furtive movement of a figure on his left, rising from cover in a clump of ferns. The lookout should've shot him without warning, but perhaps he didn't trust his aim—or maybe it was just some stupid macho thing.

Either way, the shooter's awkward hesitation gave Grimaldi something like a second and a half to save himself. He hit the deck immediately, angling for a target with his MP-5, as a shotgun blast fanned the air overhead. His return fire, a surgical 3-round burst, was lost in the echo of the scattergun, but it did the job. Nine millimeter manglers punched through the sniper's chest and took him down in a spray of scarlet mist.

That tore it down the middle, spoiling any chance he and the others had of getting closer to the house without a fight. Before the sound of shots had even died away, Grimaldi heard excited voices shouting questions from the general direction of the manor. It was hard to peg locations, much less numbers, but he knew a skirmish line was forming near the house, and from the sound of it, the opposition had no shortage of soldiers.

Lunging to his feet, Grimaldi straightened his headset and resumed his forward motion toward the manor. His comrades were still observing radio silence, and he did likewise, uncertain what kind of commo gear his adversaries might be packing. The odds were bad enough, without him beaming out a signal that would lead them straight to his position.

Grimaldi had two jobs at the moment. First, to find Bolan and spring him from whatever sort of cage the enemy had managed to arrange for him. Second, if he made it that far, to survive the fighting withdrawal from Aznar's estate.

More firing now, ahead of Grimaldi and off to his left. The bullets weren't coming his way, and he wondered if Johnny was catching Hell over there, or if a group of jumpy shooters was firing at shadows.

He took advantage of the diversion and poured on more speed in his rush toward the mansion. Still watching the trees and their shadows as he ran, Grimaldi nonetheless made better time, making up for the moments he'd lost in the ambush. By the time he heard the first grenade go off, he was near enough to see most of the manor looming through the final line of trees.

The bomb had come from Ross's sector, but Grimaldi didn't stop to think about what she'd encountered over there. Each soldier took his chances on a job like this one, and Ross had proved herself capable of handling whatever the heavies threw her way.

A moment later Grimaldi's mind was swept clear of worries for his comrades. He saw a fighting line of gunmen moving toward him, jogging across the lawn toward the tree line. It was going to be close, but Jack knew he'd be points ahead if he could catch them in the open, before they reached the cultivated woods.

He moved, sprinting toward the final line of old-growth trees and sliding into cover there, tracking the skirmish line with the sights of his MP-5. They were well within range, but he waited, wanting to make it a sure thing.

Counting backward from ten, Grimaldi stroked the SMG's trigger, slowly taking up the slack. On five, he took a breath and held it, steadying his aim.

The hunters hadn't seen him yet, but they were getting close. One of them squinted, leaning forward, bringing a hand up to shade his eyes. Grimaldi felt as if the man was staring through him.

Close enough.

He opened fire.

KEELY ROSS HAD A SECOND grenade in her hand, primed and ready, when her enemies began retreating toward the house. She couldn't put the pin back, so she followed through and made the pitch, lobbing the deadly egg as far beyond the tree line as she could.

One of the fleeing shooters glanced back, saw it coming, and called out something in Spanish to his friends. They tried to scatter, but the laws of physics were against them. Swift they may have been, but not that swift.

The grenade fell among them, detonating on impact. The shock wave and shrapnel bowled over three gunmen and sent a fourth reeling in circles, dazed and bloody. Ross cut him down with a short burst from her MP-5, then went after the others.

The two unscathed shooters were running like hell for the big house, flinging wild shots over their shoulders without any pretense of aiming. Ross dropped to one knee and shouldered her submachine gun, sighting on the leader before he could pull out of range. A 4-round burst at twenty yards rolled him up and sent him tumbling clumsily across the grass, losing the weapon and one of his shoes along the way.

The other gunman registered the hit and tried to save himself, spinning around and laying down a wild barrage of AK-47 fire without pausing to line up a target. Ross pitched forward to a prone position, got her fix and knocked him sprawling with another well-aimed burst. The guy lay twitching for a moment, then went limp and still.

Ross moved on to the others, pitiless. If they were less than obviously dead or dying, she administered a point-blank coup de grâce, numb to the thrashing of their bodies on the lawn. There was no time for introspection, self-analysis or doubt. She had a schedule to keep, and they were running out of time.

For all she knew Cooper's time had already run out.

The house loomed large in front of her, beyond some eighty yards of manicured lawn, but getting there would not be easy. Even as she finished off the last of her opponents, Ross saw more come spilling from a side door. Reinforcements eager for a piece of the action. She counted seven, knew the odds were bad for fighting in the open, and veered off in the direction of some outbuildings located thirty-odd yards to her left.

Her adversaries opened fire at once, but excitement and haste spoiled their aim. Bullets hissed around her as she ran, some of them close enough to make her duck and weave, but she made it to cover without being hit. Wild rounds peppered the outbuildings, drilling their green metal walls, and Ross hunkered down to avoid ricochets. She replaced the MP-5's near-empty magazine with a fresh one and crept to the west side of the farthest shed, where—she hoped—her enemies would least expect to find her.

The enemy troops formed a skirmish line and were advancing double-time across the lawn. Ross shifted her weapon to fire left-handed, in lieu of exposing herself, thankful for the ambidextrous training she'd received on Hogan's Alley, at the FBI Academy.

Tracking left to right, firing short bursts and moving on without assessing their impact, Ross worked her way along the skirmish line.

PABLO AZNAR WAS getting out.

He'd meant to leave with Borodin and the prisoner, but Santiago had scotched that idea, insisting that Aznar remain in Nassau to supervise Garrett Tripp's security arrangements. From what he'd seen so far, they were nothing to brag about, and Aznar didn't plan to linger while the whole damned place came down around his ears.

Leaving so soon, before defeat was guaranteed, would constitute a flagrant act of insubordination. Aznar himself had killed men for less, on Santiago's orders, and he knew that if he fled he'd have to keep running, fast and far enough to escape Santiago's scrutiny. With any luck, he might get lost in the confusion of the crumbling cartel, but in any case he'd need plenty of cash.

Aznar opened the wall safe concealed behind a painted landscape in his study. The safe contained 1.25 million dollars in cash.

Always prepared, Aznar kept an empty suitcase in the office closet, chosen for its size, to hold the rubber-banded stacks of U.S. hundred-dollar bills. One hundred bills to a bundle, one hundred and twenty-five bundles in all. Aznar stuffed one bundle into a pocket of his suit coat, then stacked the rest neatly into the suitcase.

It was heavy, all that wealth, but he could handle it—and a micro-Uzi besides, to protect himself on the way to his car. Carrying money was never a problem.

The problem, today, would be getting off the Nassau property alive.

He wished Tripp and the others well. If they could only do their job, delay the intruders long enough for Aznar to escape, then whatever happened to them afterward was none of his concern. In fact, it would be best for him if they died in battle, though Aznar supposed that was too much to hope for. Some of them would almost certainly survive, slip out unseen and find their way to safety.

He had a backup plan to stall pursuit. In fact, it might allow him to escape completely, if his luck would only hold a little longer.

The self-destruct system had been Santiago's idea. It had been installed in the Nassau mansion and some of his other hideaways after Colombian troops had cornered and killed Pablo Escobar and posed with his bullet-riddled corpse like big-game hunters with a trophy buffalo. Santiago had determined not to share that grotesque fate—better to die in flames, he said, and take the sons of bitches with him in a blaze of glory.

The Semtex charges were planted at strategic points throughout the house, with blasting caps wired to a central command detonator. The charges could be blown in two ways: by throwing a master switch for instant detonation, or via a digital timer calibrated for a maximum of thirty minutes.

Since he did not intend to die this morning, Aznar chose the timer, mounted on the back wall of a cupboard that was always locked. No peasant fool could blow up the house by mistake, that way. That choice was Santiago's—or, in his absence, Aznar's.

And now, the choice was made.

He set the timer for its full half hour maximum. He didn't plan on taking that much time to flee the grounds, but there was no point shaving it too fine. Once he had seen the LED display begin its countdown, Aznar locked the cabinet, pocketed the key, and left his study for the final time.

Tripp's people knew nothing about the self-destruct system. They would be as surprised, when it blew, as the strangers who had violated Aznar's private sanctuary.

It would be the greatest surprise of their lives—and for some, the very last.

TRIPP RALLIED A HANDFUL of men on the mansion's front porch and dispersed them with orders to scout the property, to find out what was happening and report back by radio double-damned quickly. There were no questions, no comments and no hesitations. They scattered at once and were gone.

He had saved the worst job for himself, trusting no one else to do it properly. Perry Blake was still off the air, and most of the firing was still concentrated south of the manor, though it had become more widespread in the last few minutes.

They're flanking us, he thought, and marveled once again that unknown enemies could inflict so much damage while losing only one of their own.

That one would be crucial, though, if Borodin and Santiago could make him talk. Once the adversary was identified, his name and numbers known, Tripp could unleash his own counterattack—or at least prepare more effective security arrangements.

And in the meantime, he could make a dent in the enemy's numbers himself, right here and now. Beginning with the first of them to cross his path.

Tripp left the porch and headed to his left around the house, jogging toward the property's southern quadrant. The woods had been cultivated to simulate nature, and they succeeded well enough to make observation of the grounds a tricky proposition. Too tricky, in fact, for the Colombians who comprised the bulk of the defense team. Tripp wouldn't have trusted them to guard a convenience store—but now he was forced to risk his life on their behalf.

Rounding the southwest corner of the house, Tripp paused to scan the battleground. At first, the sight in front of him made no sense. The broad lawn was littered with bodies, all of them members of Aznar's security force. Tripp looked in vain for Blake but couldn't see him anywhere. He couldn't be sure what that meant, but he knew it wasn't good.

Crouching against the wall, making himself the smallest possible target for snipers, Tripp keyed his radio and spoke urgently into the mouthpiece.

"All stations! This is Watch Command. We have multiple casualties on the southern quadrant. Respond immediately with half of your men. Repeat, half of your men from each station. Leave the rest in place and be on alert for intruders. Confirm!"

"Watchman Three, affirmative! I'm on the way."

"Watchman Four, confirming."

"Watchman Two, fifty-fifty. I copy."

It seemed to Tripp that a group of defenders had fallen while rushing the outbuildings off to his left, where Aznar stored gardening tools and garaged a fancy riding mower for the lawn. That group of corpses had the look of soldiers cut down while advancing on an enemy position. They were sprawled in twisted attitudes of death where hostile fire had caught them in the open.

But where were the shooters?

One way to find out, Tripp told himself, already rising from his crouch.

The smart way to do it, Tripp knew, was to wait for the others—a matter of moments and counting—to cover his play and rush the outbuildings with clearly superior numbers. He knew it—and still he couldn't bring himself to wait.

Screw it! he thought. This shit is what they pay me for.

He broke from cover, sprinting across the lawn, expecting to take fire at any moment. He had the mini-Uzi's safety off, his finger on the trigger with no slack to speak of.

When he was halfway to his target, Tripp heard reinforcements coming behind him, circling from the other quadrants where his mercs had been assigned to supervise Aznar's Colombians. Hoping the peasant bastards wouldn't shoot him by mistake, Tripp focused on his goal and reached the nearer of the outbuildings a moment later. He dropped to a crouch against its padlocked door.

Both sheds were pocked with bullet holes, paint flaking over shiny metal where the slugs had punched through and kept going. Tripp strained to pick up any sounds of movement from behind the sheds, but all was silent there.

He glanced back toward the others. They were fanning out to cover him in a broad semicircle. He directed them with gestures, his mercs backing it up with whispered orders to the skittish Colombians. By twos and threes, the shooters peeled off to take up positions flanking the outbuildings, ready to fire on anyone who emerged from behind them.

When they were ready, Tripp circled the shed in a rush, almost firing a burst at thin air before he realized he was alone. The grass was scarred by careless boots and littered with shell casings—but there was no one left for him to kill.

"Goddamn it! Where the hell are you?"

He had barely voiced the question when an explosion behind him brought his gaze back to the house—and a dark plume of smoke pouring forth from a shattered downstairs window.

THE FRAG GRENADE WAS a gamble, but Johnny reckoned Mack's captors wouldn't have him caged in a room with a window. The basement was more likely, or some interior room where security was tighter and his screams could be contained by soundproof walls.

His screams.

Johnny was moving even as he pitched the grenade, turning and sprinting toward a patio that faced onto a swimming pool beyond Olympic size, with a squash court beyond it and bricked-in barbecue pit on the side. No one was swimming at the moment, but he checked the water anyway, for safety's sake, as he passed by. It wouldn't be the first time some slick shooter had decided to submerge and then pop up to backshoot an opponent on the run.

Nothing.

The pool was empty, with the strange exception of a golf club lying on the bottom, at the deep end. Johnny didn't even try to figure out the how or why of that one. He focused on the house as he kept moving in a rush.

It tortured him to know they might already be too late. It was entirely possible that one of Aznar's people had been assigned to kill Mack on the spot, if anyone dropped in without an invitation from the boss. In that case, the first gunshot from the grounds could have sealed Mack's fate—but Johnny wasn't about to take that for granted. Not until he'd seen it for himself and knew all hope was lost.

In which case, there'd be nothing left to fight for but the sour taste of revenge.

The patio doors were wide open, gauzy curtains rippling on the caress of a gentle breeze. The breeze smelled of cordite, though, and no one inside the house could be oblivious to what was happening outside.

He went in low and fast, taking the curtain with him. He

heard muffled sounds like silenced gunshots as the curtain rings tore free from the rod overhead. The cloth trailed behind him for a moment, like a great cloak, until it snagged on a piece of furniture and he left it behind.

Johnny found himself crouched in the middle of a spacious games room, surrounded by a billiard table, a pinball machine, and enough video games to stock an arcade. He had the place to himself, so far, and decided to press on before that situation changed.

He was moving when the nearest door swung open and a lanky *pistolero* with a handlebar mustache stepped into the room. The shooter carried some kind of long-barreled revolver and tried to raise it at first sight of Johnny, but his reflexes were a trifle slow.

Instead of firing from the hip with his SA-80, Johnny closed the gap between them in a silent rush and slammed his rifle stock into the stranger's face. The gunner went down in a heap, struggling, but weakly. Johnny checked the open doorway, saw no others coming, and moved in to plant his left boot on the shooter's wrist, grinding the bones beneath his heel. When it appeared the fallen man would scream, Johnny bent and put the SA-80's muzzle in his mouth.

"Speak English?" he demanded. When the shooter tried to nod, his front teeth clicked against blue steel. "Okay, then," Johnny said. "I'm out of patience and I'm out of time. You want to live, show me where I can find your prisoner."

13

Survival bears a heavy price—particularly when it's 1.25 million dollars stuffed into a suitcase with no wheels, no shoulder strap, no nothing.

Pablo Aznar cursed his choice of luggage, but it was too late to amend his selection. The cash was packed, he was on his way out, and if he strained his shoulder in the process, so be it.

He could always find a chiropractor in Tahiti, Samoa, or wherever he finally went to ground with the loot. Somewhere far away from Medellin.

But he first had to get off the estate in one piece and do it before the ticking Semtex charges in the house turned Santiago's Nassau home-away-from-home into a smoking crater.

Aznar slipped out through the kitchen, wishing it was night instead of broad daylight. The four-car garage was situated twenty yards from the house—no problem for an easy morning's stroll, but on an active battlefield it might as well be twenty miles.

He was relieved to find that nearly all the gunfire was still confined to the south side of the property, at least a hundred yards from his proposed escape route. That helped his odds, but he still couldn't afford complacency. It only took one enemy—or one stray bullet from a so-called friend—to end his life, as Aznar himself had snuffed out so many others.

Acknowledging his fear shamed him into motion. He broke from the doorway in a loping run toward the garage. Each step jolted his body and made his clenched teeth ache, as he expected shouts or gunshots from behind, a spray of bullets ripping through his flesh.

The garage! Suppose one of his enemies was hiding there, watching him cross the lawn, waiting to cut him down at point-blank range.

He clutched the micro-Uzi in a death grip, knuckles blanched by tension, ready to unleash a storm of automatic fire at the first sign of movement.

It came a heartbeat later, when he was within a dozen paces of his goal. A man stepped out from cover at the southeast corner of the long garage, some kind of automatic rifle dark and deadly in his hands.

Aznar felt his heart skip a beat, but his survival instincts were still intact. He fired on the run and kept firing as he closed the gap to his target, seeing bullets strike their mark and bring the stranger down.

Except, he now discovered, the dead man wasn't a stranger after all. It was one of his own bodyguards.

The military called it "collateral damage."

Pablo Aznar called it saving his ass.

The garage was unlocked. Aznar entered through a side door and turned on the overhead lights. The vehicles, each with keys in the ignitions, included a red Jaguar convertible, a navy-blue Lexus sedan, a silver Mercedes-Benz, and a jet-black Chevy Blazer. Aznar chose the Blazer for its bulk and four-wheel drive. It wouldn't beat the Jaguar from a standing start, but when it came to crashing doors or gates, he wanted all the weight and power he could get.

Aznar put his suitcase on the floor behind the driver's seat,

climbed behind the steering wheel and gave the key a twist.
The Blazer came alive, its big engine racing. Aznar goosed
the accelerator to calm it down, then reached up to key the
automatic door opener clipped to the sun visor.

Seconds later, the way was clear. He gunned the Blazer, fat
tires squealing on concrete as he burst from the garage and
hurtled down the long, curving driveway toward freedom.

THE SHOOTER WAS TRYING to talk, but he couldn't say much
with a mouthful of assault rifle. Johnny eased back on the SA-
80 a little, holding the muzzle a hairbreadth from the gunman's lips.

"Okay," he told his supine enemy. "One time to save your
ass, and one time only. Where's the prisoner?"

"Not here!" the young man blurted.

"Wrong answer," Johnny said, tightening up the trigger pull.

A high-pitched squeal of panic echoed through the games
room. It came from the shooter, but sounded like someone
abusing a cat. Tears and sweat bathed the trembling Colombian's face as he begged for his life.

"No, señor! Es verdad—it's the truth! I swear it on my life!"

"That's the deal," Johnny said. "And you're blowing it, pal."

"They all leave with the gringo! Believe me! You check the
whole house and find nothing, I promise!"

Johnny felt a sudden, sour churning in his gut that told him
it wasn't a lie.

"When did they leave?" he demanded.

"Soon after they come here, three hours at least," said the
gunman. "Russians come in driving, with a gringo in the—
what you call it?—back of car..."

"The trunk?"

"Trunk, sí. They bring him in, then take him out again
after a little while and fly away."

"What do you mean, fly away?"

"In helicopter. Gone!"

The churning in his gut grew worse. "Where did they go?"

"They don't tell me, *señor.* I don't ask questions."

Johnny guessed that much was true, at least. "All right," he said. "Who would know where they went?"

"Señor Aznar! Ask him!"

"He didn't fly out with the others?"

"No!" The gunner shook his head as if attempting to inflict a self-induced concussion. "No, *señor!* He stays!"

"Where can I find him?" Johnny asked.

"I don't know this, *señor.* You ask a peasant where the master goes, what can he say?"

"In my experience," Johnny replied, "the peasants always know."

The shooter's attitude was desperation squared. "Not this time. When the shooting starts, the gringo comes through shouting and I do what I'm told."

"What gringo?"

"Señor Tripp. He works for Señor Aznar and the rest."

"Tripp's here?"

"Oh, *sí.*" A sudden, sickly grin. "You want to shoot him, I don't cry about it."

"Would he know where the prisoner was taken?"

Hope flared in the man's eyes. "Oh, sure! Ask him!"

"And where is he?"

Hope fled. "Somewhere outside. He give the orders, I don't ask."

"Thanks for the tip." Johnny stroked the SA-80's trigger lightly for a single shot that drilled the gunman's forehead, leaving him with an expression of childlike surprise.

Too late, goddamn it!

Leaving the house, Johnny spoke urgently into his microphone. "Heads up," he told the other members of his team. "We missed the party. They've already moved the package.

No word on where it went, but two men still on site should know. Aznar and Tripp."

"Copy." Grimaldi's voice was grim.

"Roger." Ditto for Ross, with a distraction factor, auto fire up close and personal.

Johnny had no idea where to look for Tripp or Aznar in the chaos that surrounded him. Should he go back inside and search the house, on the off chance that one of them was hiding in a closet, maybe underneath one of the beds? Were they moving about the grounds, leading their troops—or would they cut and run, given the chance?

If they escaped, how would he ever know where Semyon Borodin had taken Mack?

The grim sensation settling over Johnny was the closest thing to sheer despair that he'd experienced in years. He shook it off, replacing it with anger and determination.

Tripp and Aznar.

They were somewhere on the grounds and Johnny meant to find them if it proved to be his final living act.

Find one of them, at least, and squeeze him till he spilled his guts.

TRIPP WAS HALFWAY to the house, his men trailing behind him, when a new storm broke out to his right, from the northwest corner of the mansion. He hesitated, breaking stride, torn between the smoke that billowed from the manor on one side and the active signs of combat on the other.

Choice made, he veered off course and shouted to his troops, "This way!" They followed without questions even though he guessed the rag-tag group from Medellin was mightily confused.

As he approached the new target, Tripp saw one of his mercs stagger around the corner into view, clutching his bloody side and firing his pistol at someone beyond Tripp's line of sight. The merc either missed or wasn't fast enough to nail them all, because a burst of auto fire opened his chest and dropped him twitching on the grass.

Tripp clutched his mini-Uzi in both hands, rushing the corner and the fallen body of his friend. He slowed up through the last five yards or so, too wise and well experienced to charge blindly around the corner to be shot to ribbons for his trouble.

Not today, he thought, crouching within a yard of the corpse. "Peters!" he snapped at Watchman Four. "We need to clear this obstacle and see about collecting POWs, if possible. You ready?"

Eddie Peters hesitated long enough to make Tripp wonder if he planned to weasel out. Then he responded with a silent nod, shifting his grip on the Colt CAR-15 carbine he carried.

"Two men with you. Take your pick," Tripp said.

Peters glanced back at the Colombians. "You two," he told a pair who looked like brothers, armed with matching AK-47s. The Colombians exchanged a nervous look, then stepped up to the firing line with Peters.

"We're behind you," Tripp assured his man. "Remember, prisoners if possible."

"Yes, sir!"

Peters stepped off without more hesitation, the two Colombians behind him. Tripp expected gunfire when they cleared the corner, but it never came. Instead—worse yet—another explosion rocked the house and sent his three men tumbling back in tatters from the blast.

"Come on, dammit!"

It was the best chance they would have, Tripp realized, before the pitcher had an opportunity to prime another charge or grab a weapon after winding up the toss. Tripp lunged around the corner firing, ready to confront a line of hostile guns, but what he saw instead was a retreating figure, smallish, running hell-for-leather toward a corner of the mansion's southwest wing.

Tripp wasted half a dozen rounds, cursing his shaky aim, then set off in pursuit of the enemy, running all-out. He didn't wait to see if any of the others followed, knowing in his heart that he would be the one to bag this bastard and to squeeze the truth out of him with his own two hands.

Unless...

A nagging thought—ambush!—was gnawing at his mind, but Tripp pushed on. He needed contact, anything to let him vent the anger and frustration that had dogged him for the past ten days.

Tripp was forty feet and closing from the mansion when his adversary rolled back into view, stretched prone on the grass. He saw the weapon aimed at him and tried to dodge aside. A bullet ripped through the meat of his right arm.

Tripp lost his weapon and went down rolling, while the others tried to save themselves. It wasn't working. Man shapes were jerking, twisting, sprawling under fire. He lost count of the KIAs, dismissing them as the instinct for self-preservation took over. His left hand lunged for the pistol holstered on his right hip—and froze on a shadow fell over his face.

The shooter stood above him, leveling an MP-5 at his astounded face. It took another beat for Tripp to realize the shooter was a woman.

"So, Mr. Tripp," she said. "Alone at last."

GRIMALDI HAD DECIDED it would be a waste of time to try searching the house. He could play tag with any number of his enemies through several dozen rooms until a new day dawned—or the police arrived to take him down—and still gain nothing that would help the team find Bolan.

No. He had a different idea.

It struck him that the men who ran cartels and syndicates

were fond of letting others do their messy work. Most didn't like to get their hands dirty, and even those who liked a little bloodshed generally balked at putting their lives on the line in any kind of serious confrontation. That's what hitmen and armies were for, after all: to protect their bosses in the lap of luxury.

It followed, then, that while a merc like Garrett Tripp might be required to work the firing line, Pablo Aznar would not. He'd run from Panama, along with his VIP comrades, and Grimaldi saw no reason why he wouldn't run tonight—or try to, anyway.

How would he run?

There was no helicopter on the premises, which meant that anybody bailing out would have to walk or drive. Grimaldi bet on wheels and set a course for the garage. He knew where to find it from aerial photos, but he still had to get there alive.

And that was the trick.

Grimaldi wasn't keeping score, but he supposed he'd shot close to a dozen men so far this morning. It wasn't the bloodiest fight he'd been in, but killing face-to-face was different than dropping bombs and firing missiles.

From the air, there was a certain distance. Targets often looked like toys or models, and the people looked like insects—when he caught a glimpse of them at all. It was a sterile way to kill, like working through the problems of a dogfight on a simulator.

In the trenches, it was something else again. Grimaldi knew both sides and never flinched from either one, but it could take a toll.

He focused on his goal and on the thought of Mack in agony. He moved with grim determination toward the four-car garage. Grimaldi was almost there when he heard the door begin to hum and rattle and saw it rise of its own accord.

A moment later he was ready when a black Blazer burst into view, aiming for the gate that would allow it to escape.

Who was the driver?

Sun glinting on the tinted windshield made it hard to tell, but Grimaldi gambled that it would be someone important. If not—what the hell? At least he could do some more damage.

He braced the MP-5 against his shoulder, aiming quickly, firing for effect. His bullets raked the Blazer's grille and tore through the radiator, wreaking havoc underneath the hood. A second burst took out the right front tire and left it flapping shreds of rubber while the rim bit into asphalt.

Fancy driving in an SUV is perilous. The risk of rollover is high—as Grimaldi's target found out when he tried to correct for the skid.

In fact, the Blazer didn't roll, but simply toppled over onto its starboard side. The engine sputtered for a few more seconds, then stalled and died. Smoke trickled from beneath the hood, with hungry flames not far behind.

Grimaldi was approaching, mindful of the danger, when a suitcase popped out through the driver's window and fell tumbling to the lawn. A moment later, Pablo Aznar followed, a shaken scarecrow who bore only a marginal resemblance to his photographs.

Sighting on his target with the MP-5, Grimaldi said, "Good morning, Pablo. You can ditch the Uzi now—or try and use it, if you want. Your call, *amigo*."

Aznar ditched it, glowering as he descended to the lawn. The Blazer's engine was burning briskly now, laying down an oily smokescreen. Aznar, breathing it in, coughed and wiped his teary eyes.

"What's in the bag?" Grimaldi asked.

"A million dollars, for expenses. You can have it, if you let me go."

"I've got it now," Grimaldi reminded him. "You can carry it for me, though."

"Where are we going?" the Colombian asked.

Grimaldi smiled for the first time that morning. "It's a surprise," he said. "Now move your ass."

"A WOMAN," TRIPP said, disgusted.

"Kicked your ass, in fact," Ross told him, smiling for the first time since they'd scaled the wall surrounding Aznar's hard site. "How's it feel?"

"I'll live."

She ditched the smile. "Don't count on it."

"You'd kill me in cold blood?" he asked.

"Without a second thought," she promised him.

"Who are you, anyway?"

"I'll ask the questions," she replied. "But first, you need to ditch the sidearm."

Ross watched him ease the autoloader from its holster with his left hand, exaggerating the awkwardness of it to see if she'd let down her guard, but she kept him covered with the MP-5 and Tripp settled for tossing the pistol away, out of reach.

"Now we talk?" he inquired.

"Now we walk," she corrected him.

"Where are we going?"

"You'll find out when we get there. On your feet!"

Ross covered him as he rose, remaining far enough away that Tripp could not surprise her with a lunge or kick. She took the opportunity to key her microphone and tell the others, "Tripp's with me. If anybody wants to chat with him, give me coordinates. If not, I'll waste him here."

The merc's face lost a shade of color when he heard that, but he didn't beg or grovel for his life.

Grimaldi was the first to answer. "That's a double play," he said. "I've got Aznar and a bagful of cash."

Johnny's voice was small and urgent in her ear. "Terrific, both of you! We'll meet back at the entry point. You copy?"

"Roger," Grimaldi responded.

"Copy," Ross assured him. "On my way."

"Which way is that?" Tripp asked her, sounding almost casual about it. "North, south, east—"

"That way." She pointed to the tree line with her free hand, the MP-5 remaining rock-steady, pointed at his chest. "You walk. I'll tell you when to stop."

Tripp started walking, turning his head to speak over one shoulder. "You know, there's no way you can get away with this."

"You'd better hope I do," Ross said. "First sign of opposition on the trail, I'm cutting you in half."

"I don't suppose—"

"Shut up and move!"

The merc did as she told him, walking straight ahead, hands at his sides. Ross realized she hadn't frisked him—hadn't felt secure enough to risk getting that close, even though Tripp was wounded—but she watched his hands for any sign of movement toward a pocket.

Of course, she also had to watch the woods, the shadows and the trail behind her, looking for pursuers, for an ambush—anything that might prevent her from delivering her prisoner to Johnny.

They were halfway to the rendezvous and making decent time, when something—someone—swept down from the overhanging branch of a tree and landed squarely on her back.

Tripp heard the sound of impact, a pained grunt from his captor, and scuffling sounds of combat. He turned to find the woman locked in a hand-to-hand struggle with one of Aznar's Colombians, grappling for control of her submachine gun.

Tripp could've joined the fight, despite his injured arm, but something made him hesitate. Maybe he wanted to see how the woman defended herself. Maybe he liked her style.

Make up your mind, the voice inside his head ordered. *Either jump in, or run like hell.*

But Tripp did neither, watching from the sidelines as the woman fought with her assailant. She was quick and strong, slashing kicks into her adversary's shins and groin. The Colombian cursed and squealed, getting the worst of it, but hanging on to the MP-5 for dear life.

Tripp wondered why the lookout hadn't simply shot her, but he seemed to have no weapon of his own. Somehow the sentry had found himself up in a tree as they passed underneath him—and then a last ounce of machismo had kicked in to make him react. Take the plunge, as it were.

And now, Tripp saw, the guy was getting his ass kicked for his trouble. Blood was streaming from his nose where the woman had struck him with her fist or her weapon, and his legs were close to buckling from the kicking they'd suffered. He looked like a partner in a terminal dance marathon.

The woman's next kick connected with a kneecap and the Colombian bellowed in pain. One leg quit on him, taking him down, but he dragged the woman with him, twisting fiercely at the weapon in her hands. Tripp thought she was about to lose it, then she drove a knee into the fallen sentry's crotch and the poor bastard puked up his breakfast.

Now or never, Tripp decided.

He was moving toward the woman, closing in on her blind side, when she wrenched the MP-5 free, jammed the muzzle under her adversary's jaw and pulled the trigger. Bullets ripped through the Colombian's face and skull with all the finesse of a chainsaw, spattering blood and gray matter for yards.

Tripp turned and ran for his life, weaving a zigzag pattern through the trees and praying to forgotten gods that the bitch wouldn't nail him. Maybe she'd have bits of poor dead Pedro in her eyes, spoiling her aim. Something to save him.

Anything.

More automatic fire erupted behind him, but this time the slugs were chasing Tripp, cracking into tree trunks, snipping leaves from branches. He kept running, ducking, dodging, heedless of the ferns and bushes whipping at his body.

He ran like a madman through the woods with no destination in mind except safety. Wherever that was and whatever it meant in this weird, fucked-up life Tripp had chosen for himself.

He ran, and heard the woman cursing him as she reloaded. He wondered if she would pursue him. There was distance in her voice, but that could be deceiving, even in a man-made forest.

More gunshots. But this time the bullets were nowhere close to striking Tripp and he didn't even bother ducking. He ran through the trees until he thought his lungs would burst— and suddenly the wall was there, in front of him.

Tripp didn't hesitate. He hit the wall as if he were running the obstacle course in boot camp, long years ago. Up and over without a backward glance, and crouching as he landed on the other side.

Tripp got his bearings, charted the direction that would take him to the highway, and began to run once more.

JOHNNY SAW JACK GRIMALDI coming through the trees, shoving Pablo Aznar ahead of him. Aznar had a suitcase in one hand and a dejected look on his face. He didn't have a chance to drag his feet, but there was definitely no spring in his step.

Gunfire still echoed from the manor house, now hidden by the trees. Johnny was listening for any sounds of hot pursuit, but nothing reached his ears. An army could be sneaking through the trees but he saw nothing in the way of scouts behind Grimaldi as the two men reached his post beside the wall.

No, that was wrong. There was some movement, drawing closer. He could track the stalker's progress through the trees.

"We've got company," he told Grimaldi as he raised the SA-80 and made target acquisition with the rifle 4x optical sight.

It looked like…

Yes, it was.

"We're cool," he said, relaxing, but he couldn't help frowning as Keely Ross covered the last thirty yards. "Are you all right?" he asked, at the sight of her blood-spattered face and clothes.

"It isn't mine," she told him, "but the bastard got away. One of the locals jumped us, coming back, and by the time I dropped him, Tripp was in the wind. I couldn't catch him. Sorry."

Disappointment didn't cover the sensation Johnny felt, but there was no point beating it to death. "It doesn't matter," he told Ross, hoping he wasn't fatally, irrevocably wrong. "We've got this one to help us out."

"I told your man already, you can have the money," Aznar said.

"Thanks, we'll take it," Johnny said. "But it won't settle your account."

"What do you want?" asked the Colombian.

"You had a prisoner here," Johnny said. "One of your people tells me he's been moved."

"You won't get this one back, I promise you." Aznar smiled.

"Then you'll enjoy seeing me fail. Of course, you won't be breathing when it happens, if you don't answer the question."

Aznar shrugged. "All right, if you insist. My *jéfe* wanted him in Medellín. They left at dawn. Maybe they've already landed. Who knows?"

"Your *jéfe* would be Hector Santiago, right?"

"You're well informed, gringo. Maybe you don't need me at all."

"You're right. Fair's fair."

Johnny shouldered his rifle, drawing a bead on Aznar's chest. The narco baron raised both hands, eyes wide with sudden panic.

"Where does your boss stash prisoners in Medellin?" Johnny demanded.

"There's no one place. He runs the country, *comprende?* There are cages and graves all over Colombia."

"Your best guess, then."

Aznar considered it, then shook his head. "I'd have to ask him."

"Never mind," Johnny replied. "I'll do it for you."

The shot drilled Aznar's forehead and snapped his head back sharply on a neck gone boneless. His body toppled over backward as if in slow motion. Johnny heard a gasp from Keely Ross. Grimaldi never flinched.

"Dead end," Johnny remarked. "We need to—"

Sudden thunder cut him off. A tremor rocked the earth beneath their feet. Turning, they saw a mushroom cloud of flame-tinged smoke rising above the treetops in the middle distance.

"Looks like someone left the gas on," Grimaldi remarked.

"Right. We've got a trip to make," Johnny said.

Grimaldi picked up the suitcase. "Ready when you are, guys," he said. "This clown just paid our way."

14

Washington, D.C.

Hal Brognola's day was on a downhill slide from bad to worse. He'd learned anew to dread the telephone—especially his private line, which only seemed to bring bad news these days. He could've used a stiff drink, maybe four or five, but clarity of mind was all Brognola presently had going for him, and he wouldn't give it up without a fight.

He didn't want to make the call, knowing how it would go, what it would mean, but options were in perilously short supply. The Nassau strike had gone to Hell, and now his choices had been whittled down to an unlucky pair.

Brognola could move in and take the game away from Johnny, knowing that the kid would put up stiff resistance and it might lead to a three-way shooting war south of the border.

Or he could stand back and let the action run its course.

In truth, Brognola hadn't made up his mind yet, but he'd run out of reasons for stalling the telephone call. It was time to put the chore behind him. He could let the conversation guide him and follow his gut—or his heart, whichever was stronger.

Johnny was waiting for the call. He answered midway

through the first ring. Nervous, Brognola told himself. And why the hell not?

"It's me," he said. "I got some information from the Farm and DEA."

"I'm listening," Johnny replied. All business.

"Hector Santiago has a villa, whatever they call it down there, a mile or so east of Medellin. It's his main residence, so assume it's well defended."

"Right."

"It's not his only place, of course. He's got some kind of penthouse love nest where he keeps a mistress in downtown Medellin."

"No good," Johnny replied. "Too public."

"Right. He's also got a country place halfway between Medellin and Bogota. Stuck in the mountains there. I've got coordinates and aerials that I can send you."

"Good."

"Now for the bad news. Hell, it's all bad news, okay?"

"Go on."

"You already know Santiago's the top dog in Colombian drug-running. It never lasts for anybody, but he's in the catbird seat right now. Officially, the government keeps trying to indict him. Off the record, naturally, he's paid off anyone who'll take a peso and killed off the ones who wouldn't. He's still got opposition—a couple of smaller cartels, based at Cali and Cartagena, and a handful of honest cops and prosecutors who keep slogging away—but the sad fact is, you can't go in expecting any local help."

"I wasn't planning on it," Johnny said.

"Right. I figured that. Now, if you want to wait a day or so—"

"Impossible."

"I can send Able Team to help you out. They know the territory, and—"

"I've wasted too much time already," Johnny interrupted him. "You know what it means, each hour they have him, with nothing to stop them."

"That's not—"

"I brought Mack into this. Your people weren't tracking this bunch. No one was. If it wasn't for me, Mack would be on some other job right now, or maybe catching up on R and R."

"You know my answer, but you need to hear it anyway," Brognola said. "You're too damned close to this. It's the reason doctors don't operate on relatives and cops don't investigate crimes against their loved ones. You can't do it right without some distance, some objectivity."

"I'm doing this," Johnny replied. "I hope you won't be standing in my way."

Brognola let a silent moment hang between them, then resolved to throw his better judgment out the window. It wouldn't be the first time he'd bet the farm with a Bolan brother the only card left in his hand. God willing, it wouldn't be the last.

"No, I won't," he said at last. "Stand by for the photo transmission—and call, for God's sake, if you need anything."

"You know I will."

I hope you have the chance, Brognola thought, but didn't voice his apprehension. Johnny knew the risks; he was going through with it, regardless.

For his brother. And for himself.

Nassau, Bahamas

"SO, WE HAVE THE GOODS on Santiago?" Keely Ross inquired.

"As good as it gets," Johnny said, "which isn't saying much. Coordinates, some pictures. This and that."

They stood together in the Learjet's shadow. It was nearly ready for takeoff.

"No word on where they're holding Matt?" she asked.

The pain he felt was obvious from where Ross stood, but Johnny did his best to hide it. "Nothing," he replied. "They would have smuggled him past Immigration somehow. No great trick when Santiago's bribed everyone from politicians down to meter maids and dog catchers."

"We'll find him," she said. "I have a feeling."

"Right." His nod suggested nothing in the way of confidence, and Ross could almost hear his mind at work.

We'll find him, right, but not in time. Too late is what we'll be.

"Johnny." She thought of reaching out for him, but didn't make the move. It was too public, and his thoughts were elsewhere. Maybe roaming up and down the streets of Medellin or drifting off across the treetops toward some jungle fortress where his friend was suffering the tortures of the damned.

They didn't know for sure, couldn't be positive that Matt was even alive. But it was the only card they had to play, and she knew that Johnny wouldn't quit the game until he either won or lost it all.

"You don't need to do this," he told her, coming out of nowhere with it. "You've already gone light-years beyond the call of duty."

"I believe that's my decision."

"Not entirely. It's been rocky, but the rest of it's hundred-proof ugly, right down to the wire. You haven't seen anything yet."

"I can handle it," Ross assured him.

"Maybe so, but why should you? You've already covered the homeland defense bit, above and beyond. You should relax and let it go."

"I'll stick," she said. "Unless you're telling me I'm out?"

He frowned, then shook his head. "I didn't say that. You should really think about it, though, before we fly."

"I've thought about it. And unless you want to ban me from Grimaldi Airlines, I'll be coming with you."

"You're not banned," he told her. "But you're making a mistake."

"It's mine to make. Get over it."

That almost made him smile. Almost.

"Okay," he said. "We'd better get our stuff on board."

They were traveling light once again, no weapons to excite Colombian customs officials.

Ross had no doubt they could pick up more hardware on arrival in Colombia. After all, it was the random violence capital of South America. Finding weapons wouldn't be the trick, she knew.

The trick would be finding Matt Cooper.

And staying alive.

Medellin, Colombia

HECTOR SANTIAGO cradled the telephone receiver and shifted uncomfortably in his leather chair. His hands trembled slightly as he lit a cheroot with his solid-gold lighter. The sign of covert weakness made him furious.

He had just been informed that Pablo Aznar was dead in Nassau, along with most of his men. The mansion had been demolished, most likely by Santiago's own self-destruct mechanism. Strangely, while only Aznar knew the system existed, his body had been discovered far from the house, shot once through the head and discarded beside the outer wall of the estate.

Santiago wasn't sure what to make of those facts, beyond the obvious points that he'd lost more soldiers and had suffered serious—perhaps irreparable—damage to his relationship with Bahamian authorities. It might cost him millions to reestablish that connection, if indeed he could regain it. But just now Santiago had other problems on his mind.

And one of those was Garrett Tripp.

Their chief of security had disappeared.

One explanation was that Tripp may have been in the house when it blew. In that case, chances were good that his scattered remains might never be found—and would be identified only by DNA testing, if anyone cared to attempt it. By the same token, since Tripp's employment with the cartel was a secret, and he'd typically traveled under false names, there was no reason why anyone on earth should even look for him in Nassau.

Case closed—except that it wasn't.

Santiago was naturally suspicious—it was both an ingrained trait and a survival mechanism—and that suspicion made him doubt that Tripp had gone up with the mansion. He'd believe it when he saw the lab reports, maybe, but since he couldn't ask for tests or searches, the matter remained unresolved.

If Tripp had somehow managed to survive the holocaust, he might have information Santiago needed to defeat their still-unknown enemy. It was entirely possible that Tripp might *be* the enemy—or one of them, at any rate. His failure to identify or to beat the opposition heretofore might mean simple bad luck or incompetence, but it was also open to more sinister interpretation.

Had someone else, outside the group, made Tripp another offer?

Was he working for someone inside, who sought to bring the others down for personal advantage?

Was there some third conspiratorial alternative that Santiago's mind had thus far failed to grasp?

Santiago needed information, and they had one man who could supply it.

One man who *would* supply it.

Even if they had to rip it from his very soul.

BOLAN WOKE IN DARKNESS.

He didn't know the time, or how much had elapsed since

his arrival in Colombia. He couldn't have said where he was or summon help with anything approaching accuracy. Still fit enough to fight, he'd been denied the chance.

So far.

But he would find a way.

Unless they killed him first.

It was troubling, the fact that no one had interrogated Bolan yet. He didn't relish torture, but the waiting struck him as peculiar—and it hinted darkly at much worse to come.

They hadn't flown Bolan across the Caribbean simply to kill him and dump him in a shallow grave. If nothing else, the sharks would want to play with their food before they ripped him apart.

And information was the key. He knew that as well as they did. Borodin and the rest were still flying blind, with no clue as to who'd been harassing them over the past two weeks. Bolan held the key to that secret—and to the lives of his comrades. Even the team at Stony Man would be in jeopardy if their existence was exposed to the global underworld fraternity.

Bolan knew about interrogation—using torture, drugs, hypnosis, name it—and he'd studied methods of resistance long enough to realize that none of them were truly adequate. The bottom line was simple: everybody breaks.

The trick was that they broke in different ways.

Some cowards spilled their guts at the first application of pressure, the first glimpse of a scalpel or blowtorch. Others hung tough until they couldn't take it any more, then hated themselves for the rest of their lives because they couldn't stand the pain another day, another hour, another minute. A rugged few held on until their minds snapped, whereupon they babbled gibberish to anyone who'd listen, unknowing and uncaring if they gave up pearls of vital information in the process.

Everybody breaks.

There is no Man of Steel, no Wonder Woman. Everyone has a threshold of suffering, mental or physical, beyond which they lose their grip and free-fall into madness.

The trick, Bolan thought, would be to hang on until Johnny and the others could find him and extricate him from his cage. If he could only manage that—

Footsteps outside alerted Bolan to a visitor's arrival. Jangling keys, a careless scratching at the lock and the door swung open. Artificial light stung Bolan's eyes, then got immediately worse as someone hit the light switch in his cell.

"The mighty hero, eh?" said Semyon Borodin. He stood with two companions in the middle of the room. "We meet again."

Bolan said nothing. Silence, as a strategy, was best established from the start. Instead, he logged the other faces in his mind. The man at Borodin's left side was Hector Santiago, narco billionaire from Medellín. The other was unknown to Bolan: tall and slim, Latino, studying the prisoner with lifeless eyes.

Smart money said that Number Three would be in charge of the interrogation team. He had a psychopath's detachment and the faint hint of a smile around the corners of his thin-lipped mouth.

Santiago said, "Your people are impressive, *señor.*"

Bolan met the drug lord's eyes.

"You'll be pleased to know that they destroyed my home in Nassau," Santiago continued. "In the process, they killed several of my men. That upsets me very much."

"Before we're finished with you," Borodin informed him, "we'll know who you are, who sent you, and the names of your companions. You'll run out of things to tell us, but it won't relieve the pain, I promise you. You'll beg for death in vain."

So, there it was. He knew the terms. Bolan stayed silent, watching them impassively.

Santiago smiled and then addressed the slender man. "Eduardo, if you please, fetch half a dozen men and take this fellow to the operating room. We may as well get started right away."

Nassau, Bahamas

"I DON'T UNDERSTAND this," Maxwell Reed complained. "How can you say he's gone. What does it mean?"

Sun Zu-Wang wore a patient expression on his ageless face, as if he were explaining an arithmetic problem to a dull-witted child. It infuriated Reed, but he was wise enough to keep most of the anger from his voice. Sun and his associates were a means to an end. Insulting them could be a grievous mistake.

"I mean," said Sun, "that Garrett Tripp is missing. The police confirm that he is not among the bodies that have been identified from Aznar's home outside the city. There's a chance he was inside the house when it exploded, but somehow I don't believe it. There's a possibility we'll never know."

A voice inside Reed's skull was telling him to ask more questions. He began with, "If he's still alive, why would he run away?"

Sun shrugged. "It was his last chance, was it not? We said as much, after the raids in Panama. Tripp may have felt some punishment lay waiting for him if he failed again."

"Where would he go?"

"A mercenary with connections all around the world? Who knows? We might locate him if we put our minds to it. Such things are possible. But do we have that luxury?"

Sun had touched upon the question that was troubling Reed the most. "What will we do without him? If the revolution falters—if it fails—"

"Don't be alarmed. The world is full of soldiers, Mr. President."

Reed almost smiled at that, but worry kept him from it, stole the pleasure from him. He would not be Mr. President until his army occupied the capital of Isla de Victoria and took his adversary—Grover Halsey—prisoner.

"I've only thought of this just now," Reed blurted, embarrassed but unable to contain himself. "What if these people who've harassed us and inflicted so much damage work for him?"

Sun frowned and asked, "For whom?"

"Halsey! Who else? You've all been thinking they were sent by rivals from your homelands, but we've overlooked the obvious. They're after me! They want to rob me of my birthright and my destiny!"

"Perhaps," the Triad leader said. "But you'll admit they have a curious approach to it. Instead of simply killing you, they waste their energy killing Sicilians, Russians and Chinese."

"Not wasted! Don't you see?" Reed felt the strength of revelation lifting him, until it almost seemed that he was levitating from his chair. "They know you all support me. They're destroying you to cripple me! It's a conspiracy! Who else but Halsey is so devious?"

"You may be right," Sun conceded. "In any case, we should know soon. I have every faith that Borodin and Santiago will persuade their prisoner to speak."

"And what of Tripp?"

Another shrug. "If he's alive, and if he gets in touch with us, we'll find out what he has to say."

TRIPP WAS ALIVE, but at the moment he cared fuck-all about talking to Sun. He had a life to save—namely, his own.

Tripp had survived the afternoon because he always planned ahead, accepting defeat as a possible outcome of any engagement. Confidence was one thing; delusions of grandeur were a ticket to the boneyard.

With that in mind, he had established a hideout in Nassau within hours of arrival. It was nothing fancy, just a hole-in-the-wall apartment where he'd stashed first-aid supplies, spare weapons, clothing, and sufficient cash to get him out of danger's way.

Except he wasn't sure about the last part of the plan.

Not anymore.

The wounded arm was nothing much. He'd suffered worse, on more than one occasion, and Tripp knew it wouldn't slow him down enough to make a difference. Bandages, some disinfectant—he was good to go.

The hit his reputation had sustained was something else, however. It might not be fatal yet, but if he walked away and let it fester without fighting back, six months from now there wouldn't be a soldier in the world who'd trust Tripp with his life.

That was the hell of it. He had enough loot stashed away to let him hide out for a while, perhaps a year, without feeling the pinch. But there was nowhere near enough in his accounts to let him think about retiring. Tripp had overcome part of the soldier's natural aversion to financial responsibility, but Isla de Victoria was supposed to be the job that left him set for life.

And so far, he was blowing it.

It may not be too late.

The thought was reckless, maybe even suicidal, but Tripp had learned to trust his instincts, and his options were severely limited. He could hide out awhile, using one of the false identities he had concocted for himself, then go in search of grunt work in some foreign war. But there was still the risk that he'd be recognized, that someone with a grudge or just a yen for cash would rat him out to the cartel.

Better to go in on his own and try to cut a deal, if he could swing it. Maybe salvage something from the rubble that had once been his career. It wasn't over yet, Tripp thought—or, if it was, at least he ought to go out with a bang.

To maintain his job with the cartel—or even just to get them off his case, without a contract dogging him for the rest of his life—he'd have to offer them something they couldn't get anywhere else.

The key to their problem.

He had to find out who'd been kicking their asses for the past two weeks, and then devise a method of eliminating the opposition. And to do that, he would have to tap his contacts in a hurry.

The first three calls went nowhere. Tripp assumed the mercs he tried to reach were either dead or busy looking out for number one after the bash at Aznar's place. He couldn't blame them, since he was engaged in very much the same activity himself. But it was damned inconsiderate of them to place their own safety above his.

He scored on the fourth call. A cautious voice answered on the fifth ring, just when Tripp was about to give up. "Yeah, who's this?"

"Don't you know me?" Tripp asked. He was too smart to toss out a name on the phone.

"Jesus, sure! I mean, yessir! I thought you were...you know."

"Not yet," Tripp replied. "It was close, but I'm still kicking. I need some help."

No hesitation on the other end. "Yes, sir. Whatever I can do."

"Good man." Tripp smiled. "Here's what I need...."

Airborne over the Caribbean

THEY WERE REVERSING their course, more or less. Short days earlier, four of them had flown from Panama City to Nassau, avoiding Cuban airspace in the Learjet Longhorn 60. Now they were flying west again, bound not for Panama but rather Medellin, in the heart of Colombia's Cordillera Occidental.

Drug country.

Out of the frying pan into the blast furnace.

Johnny sat alone with his thoughts for the moment. The fight that lay ahead of him would be the most important of his life—and yet he wondered if it had already been lost before he'd even taken to the field.

How many hours had it been since Mack had been captured? Going on eighteen, he calculated—call it twelve, allowing for travel time and the attendant preparations. Minds and bodies could be broken in seconds, no matter how strong a person thought he was before the grilling started.

And if Mack was *too* strong, if his captors couldn't break him, he'd be worthless, disposable.

A day of reckoning was on its way, but Johnny's adversaries didn't know it yet. He guessed they might feel reasonably confident, despite their losses, with a prisoner in hand and hopes that he would solve their problems by revealing names, addresses, government affiliations.

And they were right, to an extent.

If Mack was broken, he could blow the lid off Stony Man, its team, and covert operations spanning years, encircling the globe. If even part of what he knew fell into hostile hands, more lives would be in jeopardy than even Johnny realized. Brognola might be safe in Washington—but who could really say. The team in Virginia would clearly be compromised—and who else?

And then, there was Johnny himself.

No problem, he thought. You bastards won't have to come looking for me.

He was strolling into the spider's parlor without even waiting for the classic invitation. He'd let them witness the effects as they unfolded in their own backyard.

Hector Santiago wasn't the only warlord on the team, perhaps not even a first among equals. The same was true for Semyon Borodin. Each mobster was a shark in his own native waters but somewhat less impressive the farther he swam from home. Together, their power was enhanced—but they had built-in weaknesses.

Mistrust, for one. The paranoia that came with illicit power, an unavoidable side-effect. Johnny planned to make the most of that and use those weaknesses to send them straight to Hell.

In front of him, the sun blazed red and transformed the Caribbean into a sea of blood.

* * * * *

Don't miss the pulse-pounding conclusion of
THE ORG CRIME TRILOGY.
Look for The Executioner #310 KILLING HEAT,
in September.

Stony Man is deployed against an armed
invasion on American soil...

COLD
OBJECTIVE

A Seattle-based oil tycoon has put his wealth and twisted
vision to work in a quest to control the world's oil reserves.
He's got what it takes to pull it off: the Russian mafiya on his
payroll, and Middle East sympathizers willing to die to see
America burn. And if that's not enough, he's got the nukes
and bioweapons to bring the world to its knees. Stony Man
unleashes an all-out assault, knowing that a few good men
are all it takes to stand up, be counted and face down evil.
Or die trying.

STONY
MAN ®

*Available
October 2004
at your favorite
retail outlet.*

THE
DESTROYER

INDUSTRIAL EVOLUTION

GUESS WHO'S COMING TO DINNER?

Take a couple of techno-geniuses on the wrong side of the law, add a politician so corrupt his quest for the presidency is quite promising and throw in a secret civilization of freaky-looking subterranean dwellers who haven't seen the light of day in a long time—it all adds up to one big pain for Remo.

Book 2 of Reprise of the Machines

Available October 2004 at your favorite retail outlet.

TAKE 'EM FREE

2 action-packed novels plus a mystery bonus

NO RISK
NO OBLIGATION TO BUY

James Axler
Outlanders

ULURU DESTINY

Ominous rumblings in the South Pacific lead Kane and his compatriots into the heart of a secret barony ruled by a ruthless god-king planning an invasion of the sacred territory at Uluru and its aboriginals who are seemingly possessed of a power beyond all earthly origin. With total victory of hybrid over human hanging in the balance, slim hope lies with the people known as the Crew, preparing to reclaim a power so vast that in the wrong hands it could plunge humanity into an abyss of evil with no hope of redemption.

Available November 2004 at your favorite retail outlet.